Fred Burnaby

Our Radicals

A tale of love and politics

Fred Burnaby

Our Radicals
A tale of love and politics

ISBN/EAN: 9783337088637

Printed in Europe, USA, Canada, Australia, Japan

Cover: Foto ©Andreas Hilbeck / pixelio.de

More available books at **www.hansebooks.com**

THE LAST WORK OF COLONEL BURNABY.

OUR RADICALS.

A Tale of Love and Politics.

BY

FRED. BURNABY.

EDITED, WITH PREFACE,

BY

His Private Secretary,

J. PERCIVAL HUGHES.

IN TWO VOLUMES.—VOL. I.

LONDON:

RICHARD BENTLEY AND SON,

Publishers in Ordinary to Her Majesty the Queen.

1886.

PREFACE.

IN the summer of the year 1882 a paragraph appeared in the *World* which graphically and accurately described Colonel Fred Burnaby at work in his house in Charles Street. 'There is a little boudoir,' it ran, 'crowded with superb Dresden and Sèvres, and in every corner are presents from princes, many of them made on the occasion of Colonel Burnaby's wedding. There are tokens of regard from Mr. Labouchere as from Mr. Yates, handsome souvenirs of the friendship of the Royal Princes, and a beautifully inlaid and mounted revolver from Don Carlos. Essentially the dwelling of a travelled man, the writing-room upstairs shows signs unmistakable of a literary workshop. Apart from the official table, cumbered with the reports and printed forms incidental to the command of a regiment, is another, with heaps of manuscript in the strange scrawl with which the writer thinks it well to tax the intelligence of compositors, and which he likes to see in type before attempting to put the final touches to his novel; for he will not be satisfied any longer with Rides to Khiva, or Channel Voyages in a Balloon. Nothing will serve his purpose but the authorship of a novel, dealing with political questions and personages. This is the *magnum opus* on which the Colonel of the Blues gets to work early in the morning, before his regimental duties take him away to barracks. His manuscript, like his acts and deeds generally, is on a large scale. There are certain men who require elbow-room, and whose height makes ordinary furniture appear absurd. At an ordinary table Colonel Burnaby would find writing crippling work, so he employs a writing-board, like a drawing-board, made out of the side of an old portmanteau. Resting this on one knee, he describes with great rapidity the caligraphic puzzles he intends for the printer, sometimes in blue ink, sometimes with a xylographic pen, often with a lead pencil.'

On the death of his mother, Colonel Burnaby left 18, Charles Street, and took up his residence at 36, Beaufort Gardens.

Most of the summer of 1884 he spent at Somerby, his estate in Leicestershire, returning to Beaufort Gardens in time to make his final preparations for his journey to the Soudan.

The night before Colonel Burnaby left England, he gave into my charge, amongst other important papers, the manuscript of the novel which I present to the public under the title of 'Our Radicals.'

In doing so, I am but carrying out an intention of his own. One of the last things he said to me at Victoria Station, a few minutes before his departure, was, 'I shall publish that novel when I return, but it will want a great deal of re-writing.'

Had he lived to carry out his purpose, I believe great alterations would have been made in the construction of the work. Those material alterations with which he acquainted me, I have refrained from making, as by so doing I should, in a great measure, have destroyed its originality.

Occasionally it has been necessary to remodel sentences, and to supply dialogues; and as the novel was unfinished, I have been obliged to complete it, on the lines which he laid down. But, with these exceptions, I have followed the original reading, word for word; and the difficulties which others have experienced in deciphering the manuscript, I have overcome through familiarity with the author's handwriting.

In going through his papers after his death, I found three letters written by him, which possess some general interest, and which illustrate his own words, that to describe the places through which one travels, it is essential that one should write easily and graphically.

The first is dated February 11th, 1877, from Erzeroum, Turkey in Asia, and was written three days after his arrival at that place, from Scutari, during his famous ride on horseback across Asia Minor:

'It has been a hard journey. Over 13,000 miles, and all on horseback, through deep mud at first, and in some places up to the horses' girths. But on we went, leaving Ismid, the ancient Nicomedia, behind us, and spending the nights with people of all sorts of nationalities—Circassians, Tartars, Turks, Greeks and Armenians, for all these races own the Sultan as Lord of Anatolia—till we reached Angora, the town from whence the goat's hair so celebrated in Europe is brought to our English markets. I stayed at Angora three days, and was the guest of a rich Turkish gentleman, who treated me in a princely manner. Then on the track again, over mountains and crags, passing over ground that abounds with mineral wealth, and, alas! left idly in the earth, till I reached Jurgat, where I was the guest of an Armenian Christian. These Armenian Christians keep their wives in harems, and never allow them to expose their faces to a stranger. They are limited to one wife, it is true; but to all intents and purposes they are exactly like the Mahommedans.

'"Why do you not introduce your family to me?" I inquired one day of my host.

'"I keep my wife and daughter for myself, and not for my guests," was the reply.

'All through this part of the world the same custom exists. Poor Armenian women! They are indeed to be pitied. They receive no education whatever. What they do not know themselves, it is impossible to teach their children; the result is that the whole population, Christian as well as Mussulman, is steeped in the deepest slough of ignorance. And now I leave Jurgat, and pass by the town of Tokat. The snow grows thicker about our path; we have to ride down glaciers and by precipices where a slip would prove our last. Now we cross the mighty Euphrates; along its banks we go; the scenery is lovely. The glaciers flashing in the sun, the many-coloured rocks glinting from above their beds of snow. Then the road becomes more elevated. We are always rising higher and higher. We lose sight of the Euphrates, which for some time has looked like a streak of silver beneath our horses' feet, and we are above the clouds. I am more than a mile high, but on we go, still ascending, ever higher and higher. The sun clears away the surrounding mist, and before us in the distance, like a fleet of sailing-vessels which have been tossed into a safe haven by the lofty billows all around them, lies

Erzeroum, which city is supposed to have been the home of our first parents. The numerous minarets and spires appear in the distance like the masts of a mighty fleet, whilst the white and billowy shaped mountains seem like the waves I have likened them to. We approach the city. It grows as we near its walls. The houses take form and shape, the minarets and domes flash in the setting sun, and Erzeroum is reached.'

In December of the year 1877 he was in European Turkey with General Baker, and was at the battle of Tashkasan, when with 2,800 men they had to cover the retreat of Shakir Pacha's army from the Russian attack.

On this occasion he wrote from Shakir Pacha's headquarters, Othlukoi, eight days after the battle, which occurred on the 31st of December, 1878:

'We have been constantly on the move, and it has been a very exciting time, not only for the Turks but also for lookers-on like myself. When the news reached us that Plevna had fallen, it became at once clear that 120,000 more Russians would be free to march against our small force of 20,000, which, owing to the extreme cold in the Balkans, was rapidly diminishing, on an average 200 men going into hospital every day with frost-bites, dysentery, ague, etc. However, orders came from Constantinople for Shakir Pacha to hold his position at Kamack as long as possible. This he did in spite of several attacks by the Russians; but at last, on the 27th of December last, they succeeded in sending a large force of 30,000 men by a mountain path across the Balkans, and were thus enabled to attack us in rear as well as front. Baker Pacha, with a small brigade of 2,800 men, was sent to the village of Tashkasan, to hold the fresh Russian force in check whilst Shakir Pacha retreated with the remainder of our troops in the direction of the town in which we now are. I went with Baker, and on the last day of the year 1877 the Russians attacked us. They had 30,000 men; we had only 2,800. The battle raged from daybreak till sundown, and Shakir Pacha's reply to Baker's frequent demands for reinforcements was that he had none to give, and that we must hold our own, as, if the Russians were to carry our position, the whole of Shakir Pacha's army, which was retreating, would be taken in flank and annihilated. The Turks fought splendidly, in spite of the tremendous odds, and struggled for every inch of ground with an extraordinary tenacity. The day seemed never inclined to end, and Baker kept looking at his watch, whilst the Turks kept gazing at the sun, their timepiece, as until nightfall it would be impossible for us to move.

'The hours rolled on, and our men died in their places. Just before the sun set the Russians collected themselves for a supreme effort, and charged our troops for the last time. The Turks, calling upon Allah, rushed at their foes, and actually drove them back a few hundred yards. It was now too late for the Russians to make another attempt.

'In the dark we marched down the plain, and mustered our men before marching to this place. Out of our 2,800 men 600 were killed or wounded, over 450 being killed. The Russians must have lost very heavily, owing to their attacking us in column with dense masses of troops. There was another little battle the day before yesterday, and we had the worst of it, losing over 200 men.'

In March, 1883, he was travelling in Spain with a friend, and I make a few extracts from a letter dated from the Grand Hôtel de Paris, at Madrid.

'We arrived here the day before yesterday, having travelled through from Paris in thirty-eight hours. It is very cold here, some degrees below freezing, and a wind which, as you know, makes the cold more penetrating. The same day we arrived we received a letter from Count S——, the Chamberlain of the King, appointing the following day at six p.m. for an audience of his Majesty. We went there at that hour in evening dress, and were the first to be shown into the Sovereign's presence. He was very amiable, and introduced me to the Queen, who speaks English well, and showed me his child, a little girl of about two years old. He then said, "I am afraid I cannot keep the other people waiting. Come and lunch with us to-morrow at 12.30. Only the family, you know. I want so much to have a long talk to you." Of course we accepted. After dinner that evening we went to Señor C——'s box at the opera. The theatre was crowded. "Mephistopheles" was the piece performed. The house was full of all the beauty of Madrid, and the King and Queen were in the royal box, and nodded several times to us during the opera. I met many old friends in the house, and enjoyed myself very much. To-day we went to the palace. I sat on the left hand of the Queen, who was very agreeable. The three Princesses were there—the youngest sister of the Sovereign, who is to marry a Bavarian Prince on the second of next month. She is pretty, and looks about eighteen ; he, I should say, is about thirty. Then there was a Spanish General whom I had known some twelve years ago, and, in addition, the English governesses, or companions, of the Princesses. Nothing could exceed the kindness of the family. The King reminded me of his visits to me when he was an exile in London, and of how he had then partaken of my hospitality.

'After breakfast, or luncheon, which was very good, and when we had partaken of some magnificent strawberries, the King lit a cigar and we smoked, the ladies talking to us all the while. He is a young man of about twenty-five years of age, dark and good-looking, tall, with large eyes, and a very intelligent face.'

It will be much regretted that a rough diary which he kept of his life in the

Soudan was lost on the Nile, and only a few letters reached England.

The first was written from Wady Halfa, and dated Thursday, December 4th, 1884:

'I have been appointed inspecting staff officer of the line between Tanjour and Magrakeh on the Nile, about sixty miles from this. I have to superintend the moving of the Nile boats in that district; and as the water is very shallow, most of them will have to be carried on land. It will be very hard work, but at the same time interesting employment. I leave this to-morrow to take up my new duties.'

On the 11th of December he wrote from Dal, on the Nile:

'I left Wady Halfa about five days ago, went by train (three hours) to Sarras, and then rode on camels here. The camels were bad, and broke down several times. We journeyed through the desert, with not a blade of grass to be seen—nothing but white sand, high rocks, and black crags. Since I have been here I have been very busy. The Nile here is like a mill-pond in many places, and when the wind is not favourable the boats have to be carried for two and a half miles across the desert on men's shoulders. Each boat weighs eleven hundredweight, and her stores three and a half tons, so this will give you an idea of the labour. I passed eleven boats through the cataract the first day, seventeen the next, thirty-four yesterday, and hope to do forty more to-day. Our work is to spur on all the officers and men, and see that they work to their uttermost. This I think they do, and it will be very difficult for me to get more out of them. It does not do to overspur a willing horse. I sleep on the ground in a waterproof bag, and have as aide-de-camp Captain Gascoigne, late of my regiment. He has just gone for an eight hours' ride down the Nile to report to me on the boats coming up. A strong north wind is blowing to-day, which helps us much with the boats. I do hope it will continue, as some four hundred and fifty more have to pass through these cataracts very shortly.'

Four days later he wrote from the same camp at Dal, on the Nile:

'I am up before daylight, getting boats and soldiers across the cataracts. It is very interesting, but good hard work. There was a deadlock here before I arrived, but I have put things straight again, and the boats are going on to Dongola without any delay.

'There is a strange mixture of people here — Arab camel-drivers, black Dongolese porters, still blacker Kroomen, Red Indians, Canadian boatmen, Greek interpreters, men from Aden, Egyptian soldiery, Scotch, Irish, and English Tommy Atkins—a very Babel of tongues and accents. The nights are cold, but on the whole I feel well. Sir Redvers Buller arrived this morning and expressed himself very pleased with the work done. An English soldier has just had a narrow escape; his boat ran against a rock, and he was tossed into the water. His comrades threw him a life-belt, and he managed to catch it, or he would have been sucked down to a certainty. Captain Gascoigne has just taken him a tumbler of whisky. Buchanan, my servant, is well and very useful.'

On the 24th of the same month he wrote:

'Great excitement is prevailing at the present moment, as my basin, in which a black was washing my shirts, slipped out of his hands, and is sailing gaily down the Nile. Buchanan is in despair, as it cannot be replaced. The excitement increases. A black on board a boat close at hand has jumped into the river. The stream is dangerous here, there being so many rocks and eddies. He is pursuing the basin, he has come up to it, and landed it safely.

'It is dangerous bathing here, and two days ago, when swimming after his helmet, a man was drowned. He had just reached it, when he threw up his arms and called out. It was impossible to aid him, and he sank immediately. He was probably caught in an eddy or small whirlpool, when the best swimmer has no chance.

'It is extremely cold about two a.m. till the sun gets up, and then it is very warm in the middle of the day. I came back this morning after a three days' excursion to the Isle of Say, where I have been arranging with the Sheiks for the purchase of Indian corn, and wood for fuel. I bought an Arab bedstead there for two dollars. For food, I live the same as the soldiers—preserved beef, preserved vegetables, and lime-juice, with occasionally a drop of rum, which is very acceptable. A piece of bacon was served out to each man, and a pound of flour as well, this morning, as it is Christmas to-morrow. Bacon is a great luxury here. I am going to dine with Lieut.-Colonel Alleyne, of the Royal Artillery, to-morrow. He has a plum-pudding he brought with him from England, and I can assure you we are looking forward to the consumption of that pudding very much like boys at school. I must have lost quite two stone the last month, and am all the better for it. A soldier stole some stores a few days ago. He has been tried by court-martial, and given five years' penal servitude. In old days he would have escaped with a flogging, but now that is abolished the man has to suffer five years instead. Poor fellow! I expect he does not bless the sentimentalists who did away with flogging in the army. Taking everything into consideration, the men are behaving wonderfully well. They have very, very hard work, and this so-called Nile picnic is as severe a strain as well could be put on them, physically speaking. Yet you never hear a grumble, and they deserve the greatest praise. My tent is on the very edge of the river. Large rocks and boulders are peering out of the water in all directions, and as each day the river falls, fresh blocks of stone come in view. I do not expect the last boat will pass this cataract before the middle of next month, and then I hope to be sent for to the front, as my leave ends the 31st of March, and it would take me quite a month to get from Khartoum to London, travelling almost night and day. It is a responsible post which Lord Wolseley has given me here, with forty miles of the most difficult part of the river, and I am very grateful to him for letting me have it; but I must say I shall be better pleased if he sends for me when the troops advance upon Khartoum. Of course, some one must be left to look after the line of communication, and each man hopes he may not be the unfortunate individual. Anyhow, if I am left behind I shall not outwardly grumble, although I shall inwardly swear, as Lord Wolseley has been so very kind.'

The last letter is dated the 26th of December, from Dal on the Nile :

'Every morning I am up before six, and am out of doors all day, either on a camel or on my legs, superintending the transport of boats and boat-stores up the cataracts. I have not seen a newspaper for the last month, and we all live in blissful ignorance of the outer world. I had my Christmas dinner last night with Colonel Alleyne. Party: Lord Charles Beresford, Captain Gascoigne, and self. Dinner: Preserved pea-soup, some ration beef, and a plum-pudding, sent out from England, which was done great justice to, the dinner being washed down by libations of whisky and brandy, mixed with Nile water. As some one observed, the Nile tastes strongly of whisky after six p.m. One, joking about the expedition and its difficulties, remarked that there had been no such expedition since Hannibal tried to cross the Alps in a boat. I expect to have got the last boat-load of soldiers through here by the second of next month, and then there will be very little for me to do, and I hope to be sent on.'

That hope was realized, and on the 17th of January, 1885, in the battle of Abu Klea, fell 'the brightest knight that ever waved a lance.' One who had known him intimately for twenty years wrote, on hearing of the terrible news: 'His gallant spirit has flown as he wished, in a hand-to-hand fight for the service of his country, and the death-roll of English heroes has added to it a name inferior to none in heroic quality.'

Had he lived to complete this novel himself, it would not have been surrounded with the sad reflections which must inevitably fall upon the minds of those who read these pages, and who knew him sufficiently to be able to trace in them that complete fearlessness which gave colour to his views and characterized all his actions; and which, moreover, evoked admiration alike from those who differed from him as from those with whom he thought in common.

There is no need for me here to add to the words of praise that have been spoken and written already of him by illustrious friends and generous foes. I complete this labour of love with a great reverence for it, which will be shared by all who remember, as they read these pages, that the hand which penned them was the hand that struck its last blow for England's honour.

J. PERCIVAL HUGHES.

56, Westbourne Terrace, Hyde Park, W.

[illegible] — [illegible]

[illegible] withdraw [illegible]

from Herat [illegible] for some [illegible]

[illegible]

[illegible]

[illegible] excuse

attempts to make way for Russia whereas

that power [illegible] sought them the

[illegible] to advance [illegible] W. [illegible] there

in the possession of [illegible]

the Herat & Candahar [illegible] for

some years past [illegible] has been [illegible] one

on sufferance for some years past

[illegible]

[illegible] result of the debate [illegible]

[illegible] [illegible] [illegible] [illegible]

[illegible] part of the [illegible] [illegible] the [illegible]

[illegible] that

[illegible] be [illegible]

[illegible]

[illegible] Up for the [illegible]

[illegible] what the [illegible]

[illegible] [illegible]

[illegible] that there will be a [illegible] of 50

[illegible] more especially as [illegible]

[illegible] almost every one in the [illegible]

[illegible]

[illegible]

[illegible]

[illegible]

[illegible]

[illegible]

[illegible]

[illegible] to [illegible] for [illegible]

that [illegible] [illegible]

[illegible] [illegible] might [illegible] the

[illegible]

[illegible]

[illegible]

NOTE BY THE PUBLISHERS.

As some delay has occurred in placing Colonel Burnaby's Novel before the public, it may not be uninteresting to explain the cause.

The Story being written under very unusual circumstances, bears traces of the vicissitudes it has passed through, and a portion of it written in Egypt during the late campaign, was brought back to England in such a state that it was hardly possible to decipher the words. Indeed, one of the principal photographic companies returned a page of the MS. to the publishers, as being quite impossible to reproduce, and it was only after having the paper of the original dyed, that many of the sentences became sufficiently apparent to the eye to be interpreted.

A page taken at random from the MS. is reproduced here, but being photographed after the colouring of the pages, does but faint justice to the ingenuity and patience spent upon it as a 'labour of love' by Mr. Percival Hughes, and conveys but a partial idea of the difficulties which he had to encounter, some of the pages being written in pencil, red chalk, or blue chalk, with occasional after interpolations, deletions, or emendations in ink—the chalk having especially suffered in the chafing of the sheets together, during their transit in camel-bags.

NEW BURLINGTON STREET,
June, 1886.

OUR RADICALS:

A Tale of Love and Politics.

OUR RADICALS.

CHAPTER I.

'BY Jove! how it blows! The heavy cavalry will have a rough passage to-night.'

These words issued from the lips of a young officer dressed in a dragoon uniform. He was engaged in a game of billiards in the Harnston barracks with a companion. The latter was a stout man, in the prime of life. He had taken off his mess-jacket, and, with braces loosened to give him the more ease, he was leaning forward to make a spot stroke.

'Yes,' was the reply. 'I hope, when we sail for India, the elements will be more propitious.'

Several other officers of the 21st Dragoon Guards were watching the game. One of them, a tall well-built man, was chaffing the players. He was a senior captain of the regiment, and of an old West-country family. The baronetage of the Digbys went back for many generations. Sir Richard Digby, the present possessor of the title, had been for several years in the army. He was not much liked by many of his brother officers, on account of his assertive disposition.

'There you go again, Doctor,' he remarked; 'your figure getting in the way of the pocket. I have laid two pounds to one on you, and never will I back such an obese mortal again.'

'You will lose more than that, Dick, in

your bet with Arthur Belper,' replied Dr. Allenby, not at all pleased at the allusion made to the size of his waist.

'What bet is that?' asked one of the company.

'Why, Digby has bet Belper £500, even money, that he (Belper) will be married in ten years, and Arthur, who is a most determined woman-hater, has offered to double the amount; but Dick funks, and won't have it.'

'Of course not,' said the Baronet; 'why should I make Arthur more resolved to remain a bachelor than he is at present?'

'I don't think you will,' said another of the company; 'but here comes Arthur—let us hear what he has to say to it.'

As these words were uttered Arthur Belper entered the billiard-room.

He was above the middle height, and well-built; his age apparently about seven-

and-twenty. His complexion had become brown by frequent exposure to the air, and a pair of large blue eyes lit up a singularly handsome countenance. Yet at times a sad expression would pass over his face. He would seem to be bored, not only by himself, but by everything around him. He had been in one of these moods when Digby had joked him as to his having some secret passion, and in an unguarded moment he had bet Digby an even £500 that he would not be married in ten years.

The bet made some little commotion at the time. Several dowagers in Belgravia, with marriageable daughters to dispose of, were furious with the Baronet. Arthur Belper, besides being of a singularly affectionate disposition, was the possessor of a considerable fortune.

Whilst engaged in outdoor pursuits, no trace of sadness could be seen on his features; but when he was alone, and for a time unoccupied, his gloomy fits would take possession of him. What were they produced by? some of his elder brother officers would ask themselves. Was there a taint of hereditary insanity in his family? for, indeed, it was rumoured that Arthur's grandfather had committed suicide. At any rate, Belper, liked as he was by his comrades, was nevertheless an enigma to them.

If anyone understood him, perhaps, it was Digby, the captain of his troop, who, hated as he was by many men in the regiment, was on excellent terms with his subaltern.

Never were two people so different in character, yet between them there was a strong bond of sympathy. Was it that each one divined the other's secret? For most men have some skeleton which they try to hide from the world, and sometimes from themselves, by an affectation of cynicism. An impossible task, indeed, for the canker remains, and fixes its roots more firmly in the heart and brain, for all the efforts made to obliterate it from the recollection.

'They are discussing our bet,' said Sir Richard, holding out his hand to Belper—'but you are wet from head to foot!'

'So would you be if you had taken a header into the Thames, and had not had time to change.'

'How did you get your ducking?' asked one of the officers.

'Oh, simply enough. I was driving over Putney Bridge, when a man deliberately pushed a boy over the parapet into the water, and then ran for his life. I don't know exactly what happened afterwards; but somehow I found myself in the river, swimming for my life with the little fellow under my arm. It was rather dark when I reached the bank, and, as there was no one to be seen, I brought the boy here.'

'Where is he?' they all inquired.

'In my room. I ordered my servant to put him in a warm bath. Come and see.'

With these words, he led the way out of the billiard-room into some quarters tenanted by himself and his captain. There, in a large hip-bath, a gigantic dragoon was washing a lad, who, to judge by his appearance, might have been thirteen or fourteen years of age.

'Ah, sir! and I am glad you have come here,' said Belper's servant to his master. 'When I speak to him, he answers in gibberish. I don't understand one word he says.'

And Bruce, Arthur's *fidus Achates*, continued scrubbing the boy, and rubbing him down with a rough towel, hissing all the while very much as if he were grooming one of his master's chargers.

'Stop, or you will hurt him!' said Belper, laughing. 'I only wanted you to bring back his circulation. Put the lad on the sofa and cover him with blankets. Presently I will find out who he is; in the meantime, get me a change of clothes.'

All the officers, except Digby, soon returned to the billiard-room, and Belper commenced undressing.

Sir Richard, sitting down in an armchair, helped himself to a cigar from a box that stood near him.

'Why, Arthur,' he remarked, 'here you are saddled with a child already!'

'Well,' replied Belper, 'if I cannot discover his relations, I certainly shall not turn the boy into the streets.'

'You do not mean to say that you would adopt him,' said Sir Richard, laughing.

'Perhaps not; but I would pay Bruce's wife to look after the lad, and would see myself that he was properly educated.'

'How old should you say he is?'

'Twelve or thirteen, perhaps; ask him.'

Digby rose, and went to the sofa, addressing the boy. To his surprise, he did not answer in English, but in French.

'You have rescued some French street arab,' said the Baronet; 'and yet he does not look or speak like one. Come here, Arthur. You are a better French scholar than I am; ask him yourself about his history.'

Belper approached the sofa. The boy's eyes glistened at the sight of his rescuer.

'Who are you?' said Arthur, 'and who is the man who pushed you into the water?'

The lad's face darkened, and he put his hands before his eyes, as if to avoid seeing some horrible apparition.

'Don't be afraid,' said Arthur kindly. 'You are quite safe with us. Tell me all you know about yourself.'

The little fellow looked for a moment anxiously around the room, and then spoke.

'A short time ago,' he said, 'I was very happy. People were kind to me. I was in a school in France. One day I was told that my father wanted to see me. I had never seen my parents, at least not to my recollection. I was taken into a little room; there I saw a man, the same one who pushed me into the water. "I am your father, Eugene," he said; "I have come to take you to a beautiful house. You will have a pony to ride, and nice companions to play with." I felt sure he was not my father, so I said, "I have companions here, and will not go with you." And I wanted to run away from him; but the old lady we used to call Madame said, "Eugene, you must not be disrespectful to your father. He brought you here when you were a little boy, and paid for you ever since." No one interfered; and I was made to go downstairs, and get into a carriage. The man gave me something to drink, and I went to sleep. When I awoke, I was very ill, and on a ship at sea. After some days we arrived in a large town. I was taken to a house—I resisted going, and called out, but no one could understand me. This afternoon I was told that I was to see my real parents. When we were on the bridge, the man said, "Eugene, get up here, and I will show you where your father lives." I climbed on the parapet, and he said, "Look straight before you." And he then gave me a push. I fell into the water, and I remember nothing more.'

With these words the boy left off speaking, and began to cry bitterly.

'We are no nearer than we were before as to who he is,' said Sir Richard. 'Do you know Metrale, the head of the police?'

'No.'

'Well, I will give you a line to him. He is an extremely able man, and a friend of mine. Go to his house to-morrow, and tell him what has occurred. He may be able to put two and two together, and advise as to what course to pursue.'

Sir Richard Digby lit another of Belper's cigars, and left the room to join the billiard-players.

CHAPTER II.

SEVENTEEN thousand three hundred and forty-five pounds, eleven shillings and sevenpence three farthings. That is their exact value, sir; at all events, the value for which the diamonds were insured. Then there are the bank-notes and shares. I think in all I might put the loss down at forty-seven thousand pounds.'

The speaker, Inspector Jumbleton, was a man of stunted growth, and about fifty years of age. His head was thinly covered with red hair, and his eyes, which were very small and close together, gave him a somewhat ferret-like appearance. He was giving to Mr. Metrale, the head of the police, an account of a robbery that had been perpetrated a few days before at a post-office in London. The robbery had made a considerable sensation, owing to the daring manner in which it had been effected. A woman entered a central office and asked for a receipt to a registered letter. The mail-bags were lying on the ground by the counter. A few minutes after her departure the mail-cart driver came for the bags, and on being informed of their contents was struck by their lightness. On examination it was discovered that they were not the original sacks, but were imitation ones, which she had left in the place of the real bags she had carried away beneath her cloak.

'Always a woman, sir, in these matters,' said Inspector Jumbleton; 'they walk round us just as they choose. If I were at the head of the Government I would have a detective department managed by women. Why, where their own sex is concerned, they are ten times as sharp as we are. "Set a woman to catch a woman," said Mrs. Jumbleton to me.'

The inspector was considered quite a privileged character in Harley Street, where Mr. Metrale lived. He was one of the sharpest detectives in the force, not so much, perhaps, on account of his own innate shrewdness as on account of the smartness of his wife. Mrs. Jumbleton took the greatest interest in her husband's business. He always consulted her whenever he was engaged in endeavouring to unravel some criminal mystery; and on several occasions her clear powers of perception—which enabled her, like many of her sex, to jump to a conclusion—had given him the identical clue which led to the detection of the delinquent.

Metrale was well aware of Mrs. Jumbleton's intelligence. When the inspector first married, his chief was a little alarmed, lest in a moment of amativeness Jumbleton might be indiscreet, and let out important secrets connected with the department, which, owing to his steadiness, Jumbleton had been entrusted with.

But if he had, they never came back to Metrale's ears, and on several occasions when Mrs. Jumbleton had gone to him, and offered her assistance in watching certain suspected persons, he had been much struck by her zeal and ability. Metrale's office was no sinecure. It had been started about three years, upon the principles of the continental system. Metrale was forty-seven when the appointment was offered him, and now, although only fifty years of age, he was quite grey. A face furrowed with wrinkles gave evident signs of constant anxiety and overwork.

Nothing could happen in town without Metrale being aware of it. Several robberies had recently occurred on an extensive scale. The thieves had carried their audacity so far as to effect an entrance into Buckingham Palace, during the Court ball, and had there plied their profession successfully, having cut several diamonds of enormous value from a Begum's dress, and even stolen some ornaments from the person of one of the Royal Family.

Then there were the daring Fenian plots. Several explosions had taken place in the military barracks, and other public buildings had to be watched day and night.

Over and above these things, there were the persons of the Ministers to guard, Lord

O'Hagan Harton, the Lord Chancellor, having been fired at on one or two occasions. The noble lord, who was not very particular as to the feelings of others, was highly sensitive whenever his own personal comfort and security were concerned. Metrale constantly received telegrams from him as to anonymous letters of a threatening character which the Lord Chancellor had received, and recently the Minister had ordered a telephone to be constructed between his own house and that of the chief of police. He was thus able to inform Metrale as to his intended movements. The other members of the Cabinet had been similarly threatened, but few of them lived in such a continual state of apprehension as Lord O'Hagan Harton.

Several attempts had been made on the Prime Minister's life. On one occasion a torpedo had been discovered in his cellar;

on another he had narrowly escaped being poisoned. An Irish cook in his service, a woman affiliated with a branch of the Fenians, had put a deadly drug into a dressed lobster, for which delicacy Mr. Cumbermore had a great partiality. Fortunately for the Prime Minister, on this particular occasion he did not partake of his favourite dish.

All these matters naturally caused Mr. Metrale great anxiety. He felt that he was responsible for the safety of the members of the Government, and of the community at large, but the money allowed him for his department was limited. The Ministers required such a large number of police as a bodyguard, that there were hardly any officials left to look after the interests of the public.

It was whilst he was considering with Inspector Jumbleton as to what plan to adopt for the discovery of the perpetrators of the post-office robbery that a tap was heard at the door.

'Come in,' said Metrale.

A policeman in plain clothes entered, and gave Mr. Metrale a card and a letter.

'You can go now, Jumbleton. I will see you again presently,' said Mr. Metrale. 'Show the gentleman in,' he added, addressing the bearer of the card and letter.

Belper was announced, and entered the room.

'I am very glad to make your acquaintance, Mr. Belper,' said Metrale. 'Sir Richard Digby has often mentioned your name to me. But you require my services, I see by this letter.'

After Belper had told him of the adventure of the previous day, the chief of the police remained for some minutes buried in deep thought.

'I should like to see the boy,' he remarked at length. 'Is he with you?'

'Yes, I thought you might like to speak to him. He is in my brougham below.'

Metrale touched an electric bell twice. Jumbleton entered.

'There is a lad in this gentleman's carriage; bring him here.'

'He only speaks French,' said Belper; 'perhaps he will not understand.'

'Our inspectors speak French and German, and Jumbleton speaks Russian as well,' said Metrale.

In a few minutes Jumbleton returned, leading Eugene by the hand.

'He is a fine boy,' said Metrale to Belper, and then addressed Eugene in French.

'Should you know the man again who brought you from France, and who pushed you into the river?'

'Yes,' answered Eugene, and an angry expression passed over the boy's face.

Metrale then spoke a few words in an undertone to the inspector. The latter left the room, but shortly returned with some large albums.

'Now,' said Metrale, 'what was the colour of the man's hair, and how old should you think he was?'

'His hair was black, and he seemed about as old—as old as you, sir.'

'Ah, about fifty, and with dark hair; now as to his height. Was he as tall as I am?'

Eugene stood up by Mr. Metrale's side, at the same time putting his hand above his own head, and indicating by that means the height of the man.

'Did he speak French well?'

'No; I could hardly understand him,' said Eugene.

'Now, Jumbleton,' said Mr. Metrale. 'The albums of Irishmen, above forty years of age.'

The inspector produced an enormous volume.

'There,' said Metrale to Eugene; 'take this book into the other room. If you see any photograph at all like the man who brought you to England, come and show me.'

'What should you say was the man's object in trying to drown the child?' said Belper, as Eugene left the room.

'One of two things—either to obtain money from some person who wished him out of the way, or to gratify a revengeful feeling. You have no idea how many children have been stolen from parents of late years. It is a plan of the Fenians to extort money, or political support in Parliament. In one case the body of a little girl was found at her mother's door. It is a deplorable state of things. There is only one way to stamp out secret societies, and that is by force; but then that, you know, the Prime Minister says is no remedy. If the Fenians have had a hand in this case, I am powerless.'

The inspector returned at this moment with Eugene. He had seen a photograph that was very like the man.

'Did he limp as he walked?' asked Metrale.

'A little,' was the reply.

'I fear my conjecture is right,' said Metrale; 'this child is not born of humble parents.'

'But he is French,' said Belper. 'Surely

the Fenians could bear no grudge against our neighbours across the water.'

'Who can tell?' said Metrale. 'There is evidently some mystery; if you will leave it in my hands I will endeavour to unravel it. In the meantime, what are you going to do with the boy?'

'Take him into my service and educate him,' said Belper, laughing. 'As I have saved his life, I feel I am in a good measure responsible for it.'

'Well, he will be safe with you in barracks,' said Metrale. 'Good-morning.'

'Good-morning, Mr. Metrale, and many thanks for the interest you take in the matter,' said Belper, as he left the room with his *protégé*. 'Metrale may be right,' thought Belper, as they were seated in the brougham; 'there is evidently some mystery about his parentage. Anyhow, he shall come to no harm while he is with me.'

CHAPTER III.

THERE were several broughams standing outside 172, Arlington Street, one wet Sunday afternoon. The coachmen were grumbling at the time they were exposed to the inclemency of the weather.

Lady Tryington was always at home to her friends on Sunday afternoon. She had quite a *clientèle* of men who made a point of calling on her upon that day.

Lady Tryington did not care much about receiving her own sex; she thought that their presence might be a check on the freedom of conversation. But on this particular afternoon her two nieces, Laura and Blanche Tryington, were with her.

Laura Tryington was an extremely beautiful girl. It was said that she was an express image of what Lady Tryington had been in her younger days. She was considerably above the middle height, and possessed a very graceful figure. Her face was not the Anglo-Saxon type. A glance would have shown that there was foreign blood in Lady Tryington's niece. Her grandmother was a Greek by birth, and Laura, with her flashing eyes, finely chiselled nose, and small but determined mouth and chin, might have passed for a beautiful Athenian.

Blanche, on the other hand, although as many declared equally beautiful, was below the middle height, and very fair. She was about two years younger than her cousin, who had just passed her twenty-first year.

Both the Misses Tryington had received offers of marriage, but so far no man had succeeded in gaining their favour; and Lady Tryington, who had been married at the age of eighteen, was beginning to be a little anxious as to the matrimonial future of her nieces.

'And so, my dear Laura will not marry,' said the old Duke of Beaulieu, his palsied hand shaking like an aspen leaf, as he put down his cup.

'No, Duke; not even you, if you made the offer,' replied Lady Tryington. 'It makes me very anxious.'

'After all,' said Sir Richard Digby to his aunt, 'Laura is wise in her generation; why should she be in a hurry to leave this home, so full of elegance and comfort, to marry a man who might turn out indifferently?'

'You don't, then, think highly of your sex?' said Lady Tryington.

'No, nor of yours either, aunt. We both build upon ideals; we picture to ourselves the person we love as having every perfection, and the end is, generally speaking, deception and disappointment.'

'Sir Richard talks as if from experience,' said Lord O'Hagan Harton.

'Digby's only experiences have been with the Turks and Circassians,' exclaimed Horace Deloony, laughing.

Horace Deloony was an old diplomate. Some years previous he had left the Foreign Office. He now made a business of society, and had developed into a perambulating journal of all the scandals that had happened, and were going to happen. Nothing, in his opinion, could go on successfully without his presence. He was of Irish descent, and to no ordinary abilities he added a complete mastery of the art of repartee.

'Horace, you must have been a great lady-killer in your day,' said Sir Richard Digby.

'Lady-killer!' exclaimed the Duke. 'He was a dreadful dog!'

'The result being that he is now a discontented, bilious old bachelor.'

These words fell from the lips of Mrs. Ryder, the wife of an editor of a powerful society journal.

She was always welcomed by Lady Tryington, because, from her husband's connection with the press, she had the opportunity of bearing the latest news to the tea-table of her patroness.

'If anything were to happen to Ryder, I would propose to you at once,' said Horace Deloony.

'No; that I protest against,' said the Duke emphatically. 'You are ill-natured enough in conversation; as the proprietor of a newspaper you would be unbearable.'

The wife of the editor smiled. She was rather amused at this banter: it gave her an idea of her own importance. Although herself of excellent family, she would not have dreamt a few years back of being the tried and trusted friend of Lady Tryington.

But things had changed vastly of late. The editors of society papers had become too powerful for society to ignore. The names of its more prominent members were inserted continually, and their actions freely discussed. The majority of people, much as they enjoy hearing scandal about others, do not at all appreciate it when it affects themselves. Some of the editors had gone so far as to have their own secret police. Husbands and wives found that they lived under a microscopic observation. Mr. Ryder was not so modest as many of his contemporary editors. He was known to be a firm friend, but a very bitter foe. As most people preferred to have him on their side, Mrs. Ryder found herself admitted into the best society.

'By the way,' she said, turning to Sir Richard Digby, 'I have heard of your bet with Belper. Will you win it?'

'Upon my word, for the last four days I have been somewhat alarmed,' answered Sir Richard. 'Arthur has saved a child from drowning, and now that he means to adopt it, my chance of winning the £500 is considerably lessened.'

'How did the accident occur?' said his aunt.

And Digby then gave an account of Belper's adventure.

'How very curious and romantic!' said

Mrs. Ryder, rising from her chair to say good-bye to Lady Tryington.

'There she goes, to tell her husband to announce it in his paper,' said Lord O'Hagan Harton. 'What a bore these paper people are!'

'But you used to write yourself,' said Horace Deloony; 'and people say that even now you write out all your speeches, and give each editor the amount he requires.'

'People say a great many things, Mr. Deloony,' said Lord O'Hagan Harton haughtily. 'If Ananias were to return to the earth, he would find himself heavily handicapped in the society of to-day.'

'Of course, I do not move in the same sphere as you do,' said Horace Deloony; 'but people will talk, and if they have no better subject they will talk about you.'

Lord O'Hagan Harton rose from his

seat, and bowing to Lady Tryington, took his departure.

'There you have made an enemy for life,' Lady Tryington said, as Lord O'Hagan Harton's brougham drove away from the door.

'I am quite indifferent to that,' said Deloony; 'my contempt for him as an enemy is only equalled by my contempt for him as a statesman.'

'How bitter you are,' answered Lady Tryington. 'People say we women say spiteful things, but we are nowhere with a diplomate or a Cabinet Minister.'

'I hope, Dick, Mr. Belper has not caught cold after his immersion,' said Blanche Tryington, who had been conversing at the other end of the room with her cousin during the late passage of words.

'No, I think not,' replied Sir Richard.

'And so your friend has sworn, like

Benedick, to die a bachelor,' said Laura Tryington. 'Whenever a man swears that, like Benedick, he is sure to live long enough to eat his words.'

'And he is really too nice to die so uninteresting a death,' added Blanche.

'Really!' said Sir Richard; 'if Belper could hear you say that, I might even yet win my bet.'

Lady Tryington's guests left early that afternoon. She took up a copy of the paper edited by Mr. Ryder, and was engaged in reading an article, when her footman entered the room with a card, which his mistress glanced carelessly at.

Suddenly her countenance betrayed the interest she felt in the person announced.

'What! le Capitaine Victor Delange. Show him in at once.'

CHAPTER IV.

LADY TRYINGTON had made the acquaintance of M. le Capitaine Victor Delange ten years ago in Paris. He had just been appointed as Military Attaché to his Embassy. Knowing that his old friend Lady Tryington was a leader of society, and acquainted with everything appertaining to the political world, he took the earliest opportunity of calling upon her.

'So delighted to see you once more, Monsieur le Capitaine,' said Lady Tryington in French. 'It is an age since we met. I had just seen your appointment announced. I am so pleased that it enables us to renew our friendship.'

'My first visit is to you,' said Victor Delange. 'I said to myself, who can tell me everything about everybody in London; who can post me up in society, in politics? Why, only Lady Tryington. So here I am.'

'Well, first of all, you will have a cup of tea. And now, what do you want to know? About the last scandal, or the new religion; about the elopement, or the wedding; about the births, or the deaths; or about politics, M. le Capitaine? I am at your disposal; command me, and I obey.'

'A thousand thanks! it is so kind of you; but, my dear Lady Tryington, if you remember you told me, when I last saw you, about all the troubles that Mr. Gladstone, your Prime Minister, had brought on his country, and how he had reduced the rents on your Irish estate. Now, we Frenchmen seldom speak English, and our newspapers are badly informed as to English matters, so do tell me briefly what has happened in your country. You know my profession, purely a military one; but it does not seem well for me, although a foreigner, to appear ignorant of what everyone knows.'

'It will not take me long,' said Lady Tryington. 'You remember that I could get no rents from my Irish estates, and that my agents and bailiffs had been murdered.'

'Yes; and the horrible assassination of the Government officials, and the secret compact with the murderers.'

'The people at last became disgusted with the Government. They clamoured for a General Election, and they had one.'

'And what happened after the General Election?' inquired Victor Delange. 'The old Prime Minister was defeated, was he not?'

'Yes,' continued Lady Tryington. 'The Whig families, who had learnt that the policy of their chief was one calculated to seriously affect the landed interest at home, and to make England ridiculous in the eyes of foreign Powers, used their influence for the Conservative cause. We then had a Coalition or Liberal-Conservative Government. I then sold my Irish estates at twenty years' purchase, although some time before I had received an offer of thirty-three years; but with all that I am better off than the unfortunate loyalists who would not sell their estates, and now receive no rents at all. Well, we enjoyed a few years of comfort and peace under the Coalition Government, but our trade suddenly received a terrible check. The fact was that the United States had paid off their debt and had fostered their manufactures by their protective duties to such an extent that they could undersell England in her own markets, as she had abandoned a protective policy, and become a free-trade country. Our hardware districts were deluged with cheap American goods. Men were thrown out of employment everywhere. At last a cry arose for Protection.'

'And the Ministers?' inquired Victor Delange.

'Refused to give it. They believed in the principles of so-called Free Trade, which I believe to be an imposition.'

'Certainement, oui,' said the French attaché, who, however, had hardly followed all the remarks of his hostess, but who considered it polite to assent.

'The Radical party was at that time led by a man of considerable ability. He had made a large fortune many years previous in a pork business in Chicago. Mr. Jonas Cumbermore watched his opportunity. Radicalism was at that time completely severed from the ties which once bound it to moderate Liberalism. Mr. Jonas Cumbermore determined to roast both Conser vative and Liberal in the fires of their free-trade principles. Apparently oblivious to the opinions he had formerly publicly expressed upon the question, he resolved that the Radical party should go in for Protection. Another General Election took place. The agriculturists, who had felt very acutely the force of foreign competition in corn and cattle, combined with the artisans and Irish against the Ministers of the day. The result was the complete overthrow of the Coalition Government.

Our Sovereign in vain looked for a premier from the Liberal and Conservative ranks. In the new House of Commons three-fourths of the members were sworn followers of Mr. Jonas Cumbermore. It was a bitter pill for the monarchy to swallow, but there was no alternative. Mr. Jonas Cumbermore was summoned to Windsor. He was invited to form a Cabinet. To this proposal he at once assented, and for the last eight months the affairs of our country have been entirely in the hands of the Revolutionary Radical.'

'That means something worse than a Communard,' said Victor Delange, 'does it not?'

'Far worse,' continued Lady Tryington; 'at least, that is what my friends the Conservatives say. But to resume. Our affairs have not prospered. You may remember how your nation resented the heavy duties imposed upon her manufactures ?'

'You ruined the trade of our people in Belleville in fancy goods,' said Victor Delange; 'it nearly brought about a revolution in Paris.'

'Lastly, to add to our misfortunes, the Irish—who some time previous were conceded local self-government, and who have passed laws calculated to drive every loyalist out of the country—are now clamouring to be annexed to the United States. You are aware, of course, that the Americans have recently largely increased their army and navy; but you will hardly believe that to-day there is a rumour that a large band of American filibusters are now on their way to aid Ireland in a revolt. To make matters worse, there is news that an insurrection has broken out in India, and my nephew's regiment—the 21st Dragoon Guards—has been ordered to embark immediately. If you will dine here on Wednesday you will meet him, and I have no doubt there will be many subjects upon which you will be mutually at home in conversation.'

Victor Delange took his leave of Lady Tryington, apologizing for so long a visit, and receiving an answer that the time had passed most pleasantly in his company.

'I must pay my homage to your beautiful nieces,' said Victor Delange, on leaving.

'And you will dine with us on Wednesday.'

CHAPTER V.

IT was midnight. The telegraph wires were busily at work in Metrale's office; particularly those communicating with Downing Street. Several people were waiting in different rooms for an interview with the chief of the police. At that moment the Lord Chancellor was conversing with Mr. Metrale in his office.

'You say it really was to have taken place to-night?'

'Yes,' answered Metrale. 'I do not believe one of you could have escaped.'

The Lord Chancellor shuddered. Lord

O'Hagan Harton's distress was occasioned by the discovery Metrale had made, through one of his female detectives, that another attempt had been planned by the Fenians to destroy the members of the Cabinet.

'The Fenians are becoming more daring every day,' continued Metrale. 'Hitherto, as you know, they have made attempts to destroy buildings by putting dynamite in the cellars, or against the walls. They have learnt that we know most of these devices. They therefore changed their tactics, and hit upon the following plan. They determined to destroy Mr. Cumbermore's house, not from below, but from above. It appears that there are some explosives which ignite so rapidly that their effect is just as great in a downward as in an upward direction. This fact established, one of the Fenians obtained access to the roof of Mr. Cumbermore's house, and placed 50 lb. weight of fulminating mercury on the slates, in a straight line above the room where a Cabinet Council was to be held. He connected his infernal machine with the telegraph wire that runs over Belgrave Square, and tapped that same wire about two miles farther off, where it communicates with another building. His emissaries were on the watch to signal to him when the Ministers arrived in Belgrave Square. His intentions were, after allowing you half an hour to settle down to business, to connect the wire of his battery, and explode the fulminating mercury. If this had been effected the whole building would have been rased to the ground.'

'How did you detect the plot?' said the Lord Chancellor.

'By the merest accident,' answered

Metrale. 'I had desired a female decoy, named Moloney, to ingratiate herself with O'Brien, a suspected Fenian. She did so successfully. O'Brien succumbed to Mrs. Moloney's charms.'

Here Lord O'Hagan Harton shrugged his shoulders contemptuously.

'You need not be surprised,' said Metrale, laughing. 'Mrs. Moloney is an extremely well-proportioned woman, and O'Brien is not the first man who has fallen a victim to her attractions. The evening before last O'Brien took her to his rooms in the Strand. She saw some coils of wire lying about, and asked their use. At first O'Brien would not tell her. She managed, by those arts which a woman has the power to employ, supported by his belief that she was devoted to the Fenian cause, to get the secret of the plot from him. I learnt the whole of it four hours before the explosion was to have taken place, and I surrounded the house in the Strand, and succeeded in arresting three of the rebels, including Mrs. Moloney, whom I was obliged to take into custody for her own safety.'

'Things are more serious than ever in Ireland,' said the Lord Chancellor.

'Do you think,' said Mr. Metrale, 'Mr. Cumbermore cares in his heart whether Ireland be annexed to the United States or not?'

'Yes, I do,' answered Lord O'Hagan Harton. 'If Ireland were to be annexed, there can be but little doubt that later on England would share Ireland's fate. Now, Mr. Cumbermore is a very ambitious man; and if once the annexation took place, all dreams he may have formed, as to his becoming all-powerful in this country, will be at an end.'

'What with India and Ireland, he has his hands pretty full,' said Metrale. 'The Irish are a terrible nuisance; but this country has treated them like a spoilt child. If I had had money at my disposal I could have picked up all the links of the chain of conspiracy years ago; but no, I am stinted on every hand, and am therefore unable to employ a secret service. Why, in France the police can spend reasonable sums, and no questions are asked; but here, if I were to prevent 500 murders by spending £5,000, in the first place, if I asked to be repaid I shouldn't receive an answer; and in the second place, if I complained I should be removed from my post.'

'It is a God-forsaken country, Metrale,' said Lord O'Hagan Harton, 'but we must make it last out our time. I have sold out everything almost that I possessed here, and have invested my money in Australia and the United States. My child shall have something to live upon, at all events.'

'No other country in the world would tolerate such a state of things,' continued Metrale, who had now thoroughly warmed up upon his favourite grievance, 'and the more particularly as these secret societies could be suppressed, even now, at the eleventh hour. Treat Ireland as Cromwell treated her, and give me the means of buying information.'

'Cromwell was a great man,' said the Lord Chancellor, 'but there were no penny and halfpenny newspapers in his time. By the way, have you had all precautions taken for our future safety?'

'You can rest satisfied, my lord,' said Metrale. 'No expense has been spared to ensure your safety and that of all the members of the Cabinet.'

And the Lord Chancellor went away, uneasy but re-assured.

CHAPTER VI.

IT was a lovely afternoon. Blanche and Laura Tryington were at Hurlingham with Sir Richard Digby. All the world had gone to this popular place of entertainment. The great match of the season was to be played between Digby's regiment and the London garrison. There may be room for doubt as to whether many of the thousands of people present cared much for polo, or, indeed, understood anything about the game; but it had been duly announced in the papers, Mr. Ryder's especially, that royalty would be present.

In spite of the levelling tendency of the age, royalty was as safe to call together a large number of people as usual.

The House of Lords had been repeatedly ridiculed by Mr. Jonas Cumbermore, and royalty itself had been threatened with extinction; but the fact that it had been menaced made it, if anything, more popular, and Mr. Cumbermore had come to the conclusion that the time for establishing a Republic in Great Britain had not yet arrived. This was undoubtedly due, in a great measure, to the personal popularity of the Sovereign, for caucuses had been hard at work for several years past, endeavouring to undermine the loyalty of the people. Tracts had been scattered broadcast in the hardware district, showing how much the Throne had cost the country. One Mr. Buttertongue had made a calculation of the amount expended by Sovereigns of England since the days of the Conquest. He had shown that this sum, if put out at compound interest, would have paid off the national debt of every country on the globe, and in addition have left a balance that would, if invested at 3 per cent., have given every man, woman, and child in Meltingborough three shillings per diem for life.

This attack upon royalty, coming shortly after the abolition of perpetual pensions and the reduction of the retired allowances for officers in the army, had not the desired effect. The masses were more loyal than they had been before.

But to resume. Hurlingham was crowded. All the Cabinet Ministers' wives and daughters were present. A tent was set apart for the friends of officers competing in the match, and here Sir Richard Digby found a place for the ladies of his party.

'I am afraid you will see very little of the polo,' observed Sir Richard to Lady Tryington.

'Polo, Dick!' exclaimed Lady Tryington; 'do you think I came to see polo?'

'Well, that was the idea I had in my mind.'

'Nothing of the kind,' said Lady Tryington. 'I came here with Blanche and Laura for them to see, and be seen, especially the latter. Is not that your friend Mr. Belper,' she continued, 'who is talking with the Duke of Cumberland?'

His Royal Highness had known Belper for several years, and was at the time congratulating him upon his rescue of the little boy, an embellished account of which he had read in Ryder's journal.

'What do you mean to do with him?' inquired the Prince.

'I have been trying, sir, to find his

parents, but have failed. Metrale has not yet obtained any clue to guide him in the search.'

'There is apparently some mystery,' said the Prince.

'There is Metrale talking to Mrs. Cumbermore,' continued Belper. 'I cannot help thinking that he knows more about the matter than he cares to acknowledge.'

'Perhaps,' answered the Prince; 'see, they are expecting you to mount.'

Belper was in the act of leaving the enclosure, when his eye fell upon Lady Tryington and her two nieces. He rode up and cordially welcomed them. Lady Tryington was very civil to him, for she had taken in the importance of the fact that he was on such good terms with the Duke of Cumberland. Since that conversation he had risen fifty per cent. in Lady Tryington's estimation.

Blanche soon attracted Belper's attention. To-day she looked more beautiful than usual, he thought, as their eyes met and she put out her little gloved hand, reminding him, as she stood bathed in the golden stream of the sun's rays, of one of Murillo's Madonnas, which he had seen in the Museo at Madrid. Whilst they were conversing a tremendous rush of people occurred close to the enclosure.

'It is only a rush of people eager to see the Prince,' said Belper.

'Now Mrs. Cumbermore will arise for the occasion,' said Sir Richard Digby; 'for, in spite of her husband's opinions, she is never so happy as when royalty favours her with an arm.'

'I suppose you consider that a proof of the fickleness of our sex,' said Lady Tryington.

'Only towards husbands,' said Sir Richard, laughing.

'What a beautiful rose that is you are wearing!' Belper was saying to Blanche Tryington; 'it reminds me of the one that Lothair gave to Lady Corisande. There was a great meaning hidden in that simple gift.'

'If this one would bring you good luck to-day you are welcome to it,' said Blanche Tryington, blushing as she gave the young officer the rose.

'Not to-day only, but always,' he answered gallantly, as he rode off, looking 'the brightest knight that ever waved a lance.'

'I wonder what brings Lord O'Hagan Harton here?' said Lady Tryington. 'I had no idea he cared about polo.'

'Probably not,' said Sir Richard Digby; 'but the same reason that brought you may have brought him.'

'And he is talking to the Duke of Cumberland,' added Lady Tryington. 'See, he is whispering in the Duke's ear some State secret, no doubt.'

'More likely some epigram which he has studied and learnt by heart, to produce upon this occasion,' said Deloony, who was one of the party.

'How bitter you are towards him,' observed Lady Tryington. 'I shall really begin to think you have been crossed by him in some affair of the heart.'

Blanche all this time was leaning over the rails, eagerly watching the game. She could see that Belper was gradually obtaining possession of the ball, and driving it out of the reach of his opponents.

'Capital!' said Sir Richard Digby. 'Arthur is playing splendidly; we shall win the match.'

'Look,' observed Laura, 'he does not

notice the man on the opposite side. See, he is about to charge him.'

Warned by a friendly shout, the young officer turned his head, but too late to avoid the collision. The two ponies had come together, and Belper was thrown to the ground. One foot was caught in the stirrup-iron, and the pony, frightened and excited, dashed across the ground, dragging Belper with him. Blanche had turned deadly pale, and, if it had not been for Metrale, who was standing near and rushed to her assistance, she would have fallen to the ground. Sir Richard Digby returned to the ladies. He, with others, had succeeded in catching the pony. Belper had been stunned, and was being attended to by a surgeon. Blanche now opened her eyes, and, endeavouring to regain self-possession, rose from her chair.

'Do not move,' said the Baronet. 'I will have your aunt's carriage brought round here, and will take Belper back in my brougham.'

'I hope he is not seriously hurt!' she said.

'No, not seriously,' answered Sir Richard Digby; and assisting her to rise, he placed her in Lady Tryington's carriage, and then rejoined his brother officer.

Dr. Planselle was in the act of binding up Belper's head, which had been cut open by the pony's hoofs.

'Very fortunate that I was here!' the medical gentleman was remarking. 'Very fortunate.'

'I'll bet you two to one he will make a point of telling us the wound is exactly like one received in a similar accident by the Duke of Cumberland,' whispered Deloony to Metrale. 'Old Planselle dearly loves to air his acquaintance with royalty.'

'Done!' said Metrale, laughing. 'In half-crowns; but I shall lose. See, Ryder is approaching.'

'Ah! glad to see you here, Doctor,' said Ryder, pushing his way through the crowd. 'Nothing serious, I hope.'

'Nothing immediately serious,' replied the medical gentleman. 'Perfect rest, perfect rest, my dear sir; as I said not long ago to his Royal Highness the Duke of Cumberland, after an accident on the ice, when I was called in. Rest, perfect rest, is all that is required. The Marchioness of Colleonic, when she fell from her horse in the Row, was another instance of the value of perfect rest.'

'He will go through the entire peerage if you do not interfere,' said Metrale to Digby; and an officer raising Arthur in his arms, carried him, with the assistance of the Doctor, to his carriage.

'I will call to-morrow morning to see him, on my way from the Duchess of Montreal.'

And Dr. Planselle left them to drive away, while he walked home with Mr. Ryder, who managed to eke out of the physician every particular of the accident for publication in the next issue of the *Scrawler*.

CHAPTER VII.

DR. PLANSELLE was sitting by Arthur's bedside. Digby rested on the other side of the couch, and Eugene was holding a tray on which had been placed a medicine-bottle and a wine-glass.

'Really!' said the Doctor, leaving his patient for a moment and turning to the little lad, 'I think your *protégé* wants my services more than you do yourself, he is so pale with watching. In ten days you may leave your room, Belper, and in two months you may go back to your regiment.'

'Not before two months!' exclaimed

Belper. 'Why, we are under orders for India, and may sail at any time.'

'Not for India,' interrupted Sir Richard Digby. 'I met the Adjutant-General in Pall Mall a few hours ago. He told me it was more likely we should be sent to Ireland. Things there, it appears, are worse than ever. Five thousand Fenians from America landed yesterday, and the whole country has taken up arms.'

A tap was heard at the door, and Eugene went into the passage, and returned with a card.

It was from Lady Tryington, to inquire after Mr. Belper, and to ask if Sir Richard Digby was with him.

'I will go down and see her,' said Digby.

Lady Tryington was in a great state of excitement. The Doctor had ordered Blanche immediate change of air. It was the middle of the season, and Laura did not like leaving town; however, as Blanche's life was at stake, Lady Tryington had determined to fall in with the physician's advice. He had recommended a voyage in a sailing vessel. Lady Tryington remembered that her nephew had a large yacht. He had lately wished to part with his vessel, and had mentioned the fact to his aunt. She determined to find out whether he would sell the ship to her, and she accordingly broached the subject.

'Certainly not, my dear aunt; but you are quite welcome to the yacht as often and as long as you choose to use it. The crew are in her.'

Now, Lady Tryington, although well off in this world's estate, was not rich. It had already occurred to her that the purchase of a yacht would entail a considerable outlay. She was, therefore, highly pleased with her nephew's offer, and after thanking him many times for his kindness, accepted his proposal.

'And how is Mr. Belper to-day?'

'Much better; he will be out very soon. But when do you start, and where do you propose going?'

'As soon as the ship is ready to receive us, and the Doctor recommends the Mediterranean. It will be a complete change for poor dear Blanche. And Laura is looking fagged, after all her balls; I am sure it will do her good too. Good-bye now; I have to pay some visits.'

When Digby returned to the room he found the Doctor gone, and Arthur busily engaged in the perusal of a letter. It was from Metrale, informing Belper of the dangerous nature of the Fenian conspiracy, and hinting that the Irish leaders might have some object to gain in killing Eugene, at the same time recommending him to guard the boy very closely.

'I have heard rumours of this new form of tyranny, but never attached much credence to it,' said Digby.

'Well,' said Arthur, 'if there is one place where he will be safe more than another, it is in barracks or with the regiment.'

'Why not enlist him as a drummer?' inquired Digby.

'He has been too well educated, and I have determined to look after him myself,' said Arthur emphatically.

'I often wonder how it is you have never married,' Sir Richard Digby said, after a long pause, during which Belper had fallen into a light sleep. 'You would make a model husband.'

A shade of sadness passed over Belper's ace.

'It is a matter of duty that I should remain unmarried. You do not understand me.'

'No; explain.'

'It is a family curse,' said Belper.

'You are suffering from the effects of your fall,' said Sir Richard; 'let us talk of something else.'

'No, Dick; I am not delirious, as you imagine. I am perfectly calm.'

'Well, then?'

'You will readily understand, when I tell you there is insanity in my family. It misses one or two generations, only to appear with redoubled force in the second or third. Why should I perpetuate, as in all probability I should, this fearful malady? I am the last of my race. Let it die with me.'

CHAPTER VIII.

IT was a wet and windy day. To make matters worse, a thick fog hung along the side of the Thames Embankment. It threw an impenetrable darkness over the houses in that neighbourhood. Few people were in the streets, and those who could be seen by the aid of the lamps were, judging from their appearance, compelled to be out more as a matter of necessity than from any other cause.

One man, rather better dressed than the others, was hurriedly walking down a narrow street which led from the river to the Strand. He looked behind him as he crossed the road, and more than once he stopped, and listened carefully to hear if he was being followed. Not a footfall fell. A dead stillness reigned around. To make assurance doubly sure, he turned and retraced his steps for about a hundred yards. Not a soul was to be seen. Even the woman who kept a coffee-stall at the corner of the street, thinking probably that on such an afternoon she would have no customers, had betaken herself to a neighbouring public-house.

'None of Metrale's men are about,' said the man to himself, 'but now to metamorphose myself.'

He then proceeded to tear off a false grey wig and beard, at the same time removing a pair of spectacles from his nose. Before this had been done he might have passed for a man of sixty years of age, but now no one would have put him down as being more than thirty. To complete the transformation, he took off his coat, and having turned it inside out, put it on again. The inner lining was of a greyish hue, and made of a cloth material, so that the coat presented no unusual appearance in being worn in this manner.

Turning on his heel, Barry proceeded slowly along the street until he came to the Embankment. Presently he saw, a little in front of him, a man dressed exactly as he himself had been a few minutes before. A woman was walking a few yards behind the man, shabbily dressed, but as she passed under the light of the lamps it was easy to see that she was young and very handsome. Barry coughed twice as a sort of signal, crossed the street, and proceeded in another direction.

'What idiots these detectives are!' he

thought. 'Here Metrale for the last three months has been on the track of my double, little thinking that the real Barry is at work on a plan to set all London in a blaze.'

Presently he arrived at a semi-detached, dilapidated-looking building, used apparently for storing wood.

An announcement on the door informed the public that coffins on the most approved pattern could be supplied at wholesale prices by Messrs. Davies and Bailey. A tall wooden mast protruded from the roof of the building. To this were attached some fifty different telegraph wires, which extended to various parts of the metropolis.

Nothing in the old house itself would have attracted the attention of a bystander, save that it had a deserted and dismal aspect. Barry, taking a bunch of keys from his pocket, selected the one which opened the door of this house.

Proceeding a few yards down the hall, he touched a spring in the wall, which opened a door the size of an ordinary brick. Taking two indiarubber tubes from his pocket, he screwed them into the sides of the aperture, and then placed the two ends to his ears. He had improvised a telephone, there being a concealed wire which reached from the door to the mast, and which was in communication with the lines that passed over the building.

'Anything stirring near the Tower?' he inquired.

A clear and distinct voice answered in the negative.

'Near Buckingham Palace?'

'No.'

'Near the War Office?'

'Yes,' the voice answered.

'Good,' answered Barry; 'in an hour at the usual place.'

Pressing the spring, the door flew back again, and only a person initiated into the secret could have discovered its whereabouts.

Placing the tubes again in his pocket, he left the house, and continued his walk, this time in the direction of Victoria Station.

Just by the Grosvenor Hotel he was accosted by a woman, who appeared to be begging alms of the passers-by.

'Take this,' said Barry, passing a coin into her hand.

She at once rose from her recumbent position, and crossed the street. On reaching the other side, she gave some signal to Barry, who followed her course on the opposite side of the road. Suddenly she stopped, and looking round once to see if she was followed, disappeared down the area steps of a house.

Barry crossed the street. By the time

he had reached the opposite pavement, the front door of the house was opened, and Barry without any hesitation entered the portico, the door closing behind him.

'Here I am,' said a woman's voice. The woman struck a match into a flame as she spoke. 'This way.' And Barry followed her up one flight of stairs, and entered a room. 'Wait one moment,' she said; 'I will get rid of these clothes.'

She entered an adjoining room, and in a few minutes returned to Barry.

No one, not even Barry himself, would have recognised in the well-dressed young man of twenty-two years, who now entered the room, the tattered hag who had asked alms of the passers-by.

'Capital!' said Barry, laughing. 'Metrale thinks his women-detectives wonderfully clever, but they are children compared with ours, Maggie.'

'Where are you going to-night?' said the other.

'To Metrale's. He has a party in Harley Street. Several Cabinet Ministers will be there, and not a few diplomates. I know the French Military Attaché, from meeting him at my club. He thinks I am a Canadian, and it is with him I am going. O'Hagan Harton and Mr. Cumbermore will be there.'

'A nicely arranged programme, to be turned to some good, I doubt not,' answered the other.

'Yes; I mean to take a run through the thieves' quarters with one of Metrale's men. You may happen to discover one or two informers.'

'Have you heard anything more of Eugene?'

'He is still with Belper; but his uncle, who has learnt the fate we had prepared for the boy, ignores our threats. He received an anonymous letter the day after the event, telling him to look in the *Scrawler*, and he would learn how nearly Eugene's life had paid for his opposition to our cause.'

'It is a pity Eugene's mother is dead,' was the answer. 'It is the soft hearts of the women we should work upon. If she were alive, and believed her son in danger of death by fire, we might count upon the old lord's influence against us being at an end.'

'Leave a woman to break a woman's heart,' thought Barry, as he parted from his accomplice.

Barry mounted to the attics of the house. He placed a hand-ladder under a window in the centre of the ceiling. With some little difficulty he succeeded in opening the shutter and climbing on to the roof. He cautiously made his way along the house-tops for some distance, crawling where the slanting roof precluded the possibility of standing on his feet, and at times steadying himself against a chimney. In less than ten minutes he reached a house that had, to all appearances, been recently constructed. Approaching a window with as little noise as possible, he looked through the glass. Several people were in a room below. After scanning their countenances for a few minutes, Barry tapped three times on the slates. In answer to the signal, a ladder was drawn from one side of the garret wall and placed under the window. In a few seconds Barry had descended by the ladder into the room.

'You are all here?' he inquired.

'No, master; Maggie is missing.'

'I have seen her, Mike,' Barry replied; 'she has her orders. I have some serious business to report to-night. Be seated. You know that our plan to destroy Mr. Cumbermore's house failed, and that several of our men are in custody; but one thing I think you have yet to learn—how Metrale discovered our plot. A traitor has been in our midst,' he continued sternly. 'He sold us, not for gold, but for a woman's embraces; for a thing as fickle as public opinion in this country, which lauds a man to the skies in one moment, and hoots him down without a hearing the next.'

'Who is the traitor?' exclaimed two or three fiercely.

'Ay, tell us the traitor's name!' shouted Mike Lambish.

'It is useless at present to let you know,' said Barry. 'He suffers with the rest in prison; perhaps he may divulge more of our plans that we have confided to him. I mention the fact to put you on your guard, and to remind you of the oaths you took as members of this Association, that the most fearful death the ingenuity of man can devise shall be the punishment of all who betray their associates.'

Barry now turned to his lieutenant.

'Have you,' he said, 'executed my orders?'

'Yes,' was the reply; 'all but one. We have been unable as yet to re-capture Eugene.'

'That should not be a difficult task,' said Barry.

'What report have you to make of Mr. Cumbermore, Michael?' he continued, addressing another of the circle.

'That he is not to be reached through the affections, sir. He loves neither woman nor child more than himself.'

'When do the steamers start for Dublin with English reinforcements?'

'To-morrow evening,' answered another, who had been ordered to investigate the subject.

'How did you obtain your information?' said the chief.

'Through a woman in the telegraph office; but not to rely solely on a woman's word, I have corroborated her statement by tapping the wire, and reading the return message which passed an hour ago from the Colonel of the 21st Dragoon Guards to the War Office. The *City of Rome* will take the troops.'

'Are any of our people amongst the crew?'

'Only one; he is below, if you would like to see him.'

'Bring him here,' said the chief, at the same time placing a black mask on his face, the other conspirators following his example.

The man was brought in.

'You know the value of your oath ?' said the Fenian leader to him.

'Yes,' replied the man, seemingly much alarmed.

'You sail in the *City of Rome* to-morrow.

'Yes,' answered the man timidly; 'but you do not wish anyone else poisoned ?'

'No,' said Barry; 'on this occasion I shall be satisfied if you will take with you as kitchen lad during the passage a young fellow in whom I am interested.'

'No more deaths, I trust !' said the man, shivering.

'Silence, fool! if it be necessary to wade knee-deep in English blood, we must do so for Ireland's sake.'

'Ireland for ever !' shouted all the Fenians; and the cook, led away by the enthusiasm of the moment, joined feebly in the cry.

He was a mulatto, and had been a cook in Dublin for some years, where he had become affiliated to the Fenian Association. He was of a cowardly disposition, and when aware of his fate if he betrayed his comrades, he had been easily induced to obey the orders of his chiefs. A few months before this meeting he had received instructions to poison the Chief Secretary for Ireland, in whose household he was employed. The official, however, did not fall into the trap set for him, but his unfortunate wife had done so, and had died in great agonies. The mulatto, at once suspected, had been able to clear himself from the accusation, and an innocent man suffered in his place. This crime placed the wretched mulatto more in the Fenians' power than he had been before.

'There are no further orders for to-day,' said Barry, to his other followers; and, turning once more to the cook, he added: 'Remember, you expect a kitchen lad on board the *City of Rome*; he will give you the password. Now go.'

Soon afterwards the conspirators separated, several of them making their exit by the roof, and taking the course their chief had done before. Barry waited a few minutes after his followers had departed. Lifting up a plank in the floor, he took from beneath it some attire that from its appearance seemed at one time to have belonged to a stone-mason. Rapidly dressing himself in these garments, he descended the staircase and walked out into the street below.

CHAPTER IX.

A NUMBER of carriages were blocking the way in Harley Street. Some of the footmen, by the strange cockades they wore, were evidently servants of foreigners. Link-men were busy calling up broughams, and making way for their owners to pass through the crowd that blocked the entrance to Mr. Metrale's house. It was the first time that season that the Chief of the Police had thrown open his salon. Almost every well-known man in London had received an invitation. Ambassadors jostled with actors; the Head of the Fire Brigade with the Commander-in-Chief; the Archbishop of Canterbury with Mr. Bullneck, the infidel; Professors of Philosophy with High Church curates; authors with artists.

It was a strange assembly.

Metrale's parties were considered to be the most entertaining of their kind in London. 'Smoke and talk' were printed on the cards of invitation that he sent out, and talk his guests did on every conceivable topic, and helped themselves to the choicest regalias, which were ever at hand. Downstairs, in a large supper-room, a light but substantial repast was always upon the table. The attractions above were, however, greater than to allow of justice being done to the viands.

A well-known actor began to recite a short but excellent piece. The burst of applause which followed his effort was a proof of its favourable reception.

Two young men were standing close to the performer. One of them wore the ribbon of the Legion of Honour in his coat. As Metrale advanced to meet the actor, this gentleman moved forward, and shaking the Chief of the Police by the hand, asked to be allowed to introduce his friend Mr. Monier Ballard, a Canadian gentleman.

'Certainly—with pleasure.'

And the Chief of the Fenians was presented to the Chief of the Police.

'I have come to study your interesting customs,' said Monier Ballard.

'In any way that I can assist you in your study, I shall be pleased.'

'Thanks; I shall remind you of your promise.'

'I will make a note of it, Mr. Ballard. Your address is ?'

'Alcibiades Club, Piccadilly.'

And with a pleasant bow, Mr. Metrale moved away to speak with other guests.

Sir Richard Digby approached the Frenchman.

'I am so pleased to meet you,' said the French Attaché. 'I hardly know anyone here, and yet I am acting as cicerone to my friend Mr. Monier Ballard. Let me present him to you.'

'By all means,' said Digby. The introduction then took place.

'Now,' said Victor Delange, 'tell me what celebrities are here. That tall, pale, but somewhat stout gentleman, for instance; where have I met him ?'

'That is Ricardius, the President of the Alcibiades Club. He is quite a character, and is talking to Wild Thyne, the cynic of the period. Let us join them.'

After an introduction of the two gentlemen to the party, Ricardius observed :

'We were having an extremely illuminating discussion. It will be interesting, M. Victor, to hear your opinion on the subject.'

'Two to one the question is about the women,' said Deloony, coming up at the time.

'You are right,' said Wild Thyne. 'They bring us into the world, cause most of our misfortunes in it, and kill more of us than diseases and doctors together. Ricardius wishes to have women admitted into the Alcibiades.'

'Only divorced and unmarried women,' said Ricardius.

'I tell him,' continued Wild Thyne, 'we shall all be set by the ears in less than a week, if his idea is carried into effect. They will want representatives on the committee, and will blackball, perhaps, the most agreeable men.'

'Yet you are for women sitting at Westminster,' said Digby. 'If that principle is correct, why should you object to them in your club?

'I will tell you,' answered Wild Thyne: 'I admire a beautiful creature who is for woman's rights, and I flatter her by taking up the question. I know it will never be carried, so what harm is done.'

'Then you believe in the tender passion?' said Digby.

'No, only in self-interest. Metrale does not love any of us, but we make his parties go pleasantly. He invites you and me. We eat his oysters and drink his Pommery. Reciprocity of interest. Do you think Lord O'Hagan Harton cares two oyster-shells for Metrale, or Metrale for him? No. The Lord Chancellor values his personal safety, and if he honours Metrale by his presence here, more care is used to guard him from the Fenians. Metrale, again, hopes for an increase of salary out of the taxpayers through the Minister. Wheels within wheels. Reciprocity of interest, gentlemen ; nothing more.'

With these concluding words Wild Thyne turned on his heel, and walked to another part of the room.

'A queer character,' said Deloony, laughing.

'Yes,' said Mr. Ryder, who had heard the last words of Wild Thyne; 'as Diogenes was vain of his tub, so he is proud of his cynicism.'

'He is a good-hearted fellow,' added Digby; 'although he prefers to be credited with half the crimes in the Newgate Calendar rather than to hear one of his good actions repeated.'

Meantime Metrale, who had been

walking among his guests, recognised Digby, and advanced towards him.

'So you sail to-morrow?' said Metrale.

'Yes,' replied the Baronet. 'We have only this afternoon received our orders, but I could not leave without coming here to thank you for your kindness to Belper.'

'I hope he is better.'

'Yes; but he will not be able to move with the regiment. Eugene will go with his soldier servant to Dublin with Belper's luggage.'

'I congratulate you on going to the seat of war,' said Victor Delange.

'There is, I fear, little to congratulate us upon,' said Sir Richard; 'it is a miserable affair.'

'The conspiracy should have been nipped in the bud,' said Metrale.

'Naturally,' added Sir Richard; 'and if, before the leaders of the Irish steeped themselves to the lips in treason, martial law had been proclaimed, the Fenian movement would have been long ago at an end. Moreover, Ireland should have been temporarily deprived of her Members of Parliament.'

'But would that have put an end to the secret societies?' said the Canadian.

'No,' said Metrale, 'nothing will put an end to them, save money and counter secret societies. But I have a plan which I think will be the means of destroying the traitors;' and he turned once more to his other guests.

The Duke of Beaulieu entered the room at that moment. He had just returned from the House of Commons, where he had been listening to an important debate. It had been brought on by Mr. Bullneck, who had moved that, as England was a peace-loving nation, and as the inhabitants of India were now trying to retake from us what we had taken from them by force and treachery in the last century, it was expedient that British forces be immediately withdrawn from Hindostan.

'You know,' said O'Hagan Harton to Metrale, 'for a long time past there has been a cry that India costs us more than she brings us in ; not that this really is the case, but it was felt that it would be convenient to have an excuse for retiring to make way for Russia, who is always ready to advance. With Russia in possession of a railroad from the Caspian to Herat and Candahar, our position in India has been one of sufferance for some years past.'

'What was the result of the debate ?' said Metrale ; 'did they divide ?'

'Yes,' said the Duke of Beaulieu ; 'and the curious part of the story has to come. You remember it was decided a few months ago that all voting in the House of Commons should be by ballot. Since then it has been extremely difficult for the whips to estimate what the majority would be. This evening Snapper, the whip, informed me that in all probability there would be a majority of fifty for Bullneck. Almost everyone spoke in favour of the motion; but after the votes had been counted it was found that not more than twenty members were voting with Bullneck.'

'The fact is,' said Lord O'Hagan Harton, 'members are afraid of their constituencies, and vote in favour of measures of which they quite disapprove.'

'Then India is not to be given up?' said Sir Richard Digby.

'Thank heaven, there is still some little patriotism left in the House!' said Metralc.

'Oh, we are going to the dogs as fast as we can!' said the Duke.

'Any more news about Ireland?' asked Sir Richard Digby.

'The old story. Only a few more women and children burnt to death,' replied the Lord Chancellor; 'and the Fenians are reported to have landed from America.'

'When will there be an end of it?' said Sir Richard Digby despairingly.

By this time the company had broken up into little knots for conversation. The smoke was so thick that it was difficult to recognise anyone across the room, and it enabled the Canadian gentleman to pass about unobserved, and gather from the fragments of conversation some valuable information.

He and Captain Victor Delange were almost the last to depart from a room which that evening had held beneath its roof representatives of art, science, literature and politics, and even of Fenianism itself.

CHAPTER X.

REVEILLE had sounded at daylight in the Harnston Barracks. Everything was in preparation for an early march. A number of large vans, drawn by horses, were filled with the penates of the men and officers of the 21st Dragoon Guards. Soldiers in their shirt-sleeves were giving the last rub-down to their troop horses. Women were trying to discover a spare place for some small piece of furniture they could not find it in their heart to abandon ; and there was the usual apparent confusion which is to be seen in every barracks in the kingdom the last three hours before a regiment shifts its quarters.

'I shall not be sorry when we are out of this,' said stout Dr. Allenby to his friend Tom Ostend. 'In the last half-hour I have been sent for to the orderly-room at least a dozen times. The married women and children give so much trouble. The Adjutant says that these people are under my special charge, and that I must see in what order they leave their quarters, and that their rooms are left in a proper sanitary condition before we march.'

'You will have old Titus down on you if you are not careful. He told me he intended going round the barracks himself. He is in one of his tantrums this morning; probably because her ladyship has announced her intention of embarking with him.'

'If he bullies us,' said the Doctor, 'there

is one consolation—he gets well bullied himself.'

'The old man looked quite pleased,' said Ostend, 'when he received the telegram ordering us to start at once for Dublin; and did you see how his face fell when Lady Mulligan announced her intention of accompanying him?'

'There he is,' said the Doctor, 'in a fidget, as usual. He is gesticulating at the Adjutant. I suppose I must go and look after these confounded women.'

'And I to my troop stable,' added Captain Ostend.

Sir Titus Mulligan, who commanded the 21st Dragoon Guards, was a short slim man. His bronzed face and many medals showed that he had seen much service in many different parts of the globe. He was about forty-seven years of age, and was looked upon as a martinet by his regiment.

In private life he was agreeable and pleasant enough, but in barracks he was extremely strict. Before his marriage to Mrs. O'Donnell, a widow lady about four years younger than himself, he had been frequently on leave of absence for weeks at a time, leaving the management of the barracks in the hands of his second in command and his Adjutant. But since his marriage, whether it was to escape from Lady Mulligan, or from some more chivalrous cause, he had hardly ever been out of the barrack-yard. The men were kept burnishing steel accoutrements from morning to night.

Sir Titus had been quartered for some time in India, and he now found that the cold east winds of England were very trying to his liver. He had been hoping to receive instructions to embark his regiment for Hindostan, but the telegram from the

War Office had countermanded the original orders, and he was forced to proceed to Ireland. To crown his misfortunes, Lady Mulligan, who never let him have a moment's peace, and who was seldom out of the barracks, had announced her intention of accompanying him. India, he knew, would have been too remote a quarter of the globe for his wife; but Dublin was quite another place, and there would in all probability be entertainments at the Local Self-Government Lodge of a sufficiently exclusive order to allow of her presence there.

Just outside the barrack-gates stood a detached villa, which had been rented for six months by Sir Titus, and before the door of this residence stood three enormous vans filled with the household goods of Lady Mulligan. She was screaming in a high key from a window to some men engaged in packing boxes of glass and china, that they were not to economize their straw.

Meanwhile, her husband was striding round the barracks finding fault with his men for the most trivial things.

'Such things never occurred in my time, sir,' he was shouting to Captain Ostend. 'When I was subaltern there were no competitive examinations. We had not to learn Chaucer by heart, or digest Shakespeare; but we had to study cleanliness. Look at that horse! he has not been properly groomed; put your finger on the animal's shoulder. Not there, sir. God! the man doesn't know his shoulder from his hoof.'

'Damn it, there's no pleasing him now!' said Captain Ostend, as the commander passed on. 'If it were not for Adjutant Careful, who keeps him in some sort of bounds, I should have sent my papers in long ago.'

Adjutant Careful was a very different man from his chief. He was the only officer in the regiment of whom Lady Mulligan stood in awe. Careful's calm and phlegmatic manner had the effect of cold water on her gushing temperament. She did not fail to urge her husband to use his influence against Careful. His Adjutant, however, gave him no opportunity to find any fault with the performance of his military duties. He knew his work quite as well, if not better than his Colonel, and was twice as popular as that officer in the regiment.

The Colonel had duly visited the stables, and was on the point of returning to the mess-room, when Dr. Allenby appeared.

'I have inspected all the married people's quarters,' said the Doctor.

As the Doctor was speaking an open carriage entered the barrack-yard, containing the Colonel's wife and her sister.

'Dr. Allenby!' exclaimed Lady Mulligan. In spite of his corpulence, the Doctor ran rather than walked to the barouche.

Lady Mulligan graciously extended her hand.

'Oh, Allenby,' she said, 'it has occurred to me that I should like to look round the married people's quarters.'

'I was just about to show the Colonel over them, but he has gone away for a moment,' answered Dr. Allenby.

'Oh, we need not wait for him,' said Lady Mulligan, 'if you will accompany us.'

The Doctor did not hesitate. Lady Mulligan ruled Sir Titus, and Sir Titus ruled the regiment, so Lady Mulligan may have been said to rule them both.

Great was the consternation amongst

the soldiers' wives when they saw her ladyship approaching. Many attempts were made to hide from her eagle-eye small heaps of rubbish, broken glass, etc., the accumulation of the last six months. Amongst other rooms which more particularly offended the gaze of Lady Mulligan was one tenanted by Bruce's wife. The poor woman had Eugene to attend to, and her husband was busy looking after his master's luggage.

'Very untidy,' said Lady Mulligan, as she entered; 'and you, too, the wife of an officer's servant! Who is the boy?' she added, pointing to Eugene.

'He is Captain Belper's, my lady.'

'Captain Belper's!' screamed Lady Mulligan; 'the monster isn't married!'

'Allow me to explain,' said Dr. Allenby. And the Doctor told Lady Mulligan the circumstances of the case.

'And so you are going to take him with you to Ireland?' said her ladyship.

'Yes, my lady,' answered Mrs. Bruce; 'that is, if the Colonel—leastways, your ladyship—has no objection.'

'He may go,' said Lady Mulligan, sweeping out of the room, and joined in the hall by Sir Titus.

An hour later the trumpeter had sounded a general parade, and Sir Titus and his Adjutant were riding by the ranks of the 21st.

Her ladyship was giving some instructions to the bandmaster from her carriage-door.

'What shall you play when you march out of barracks?' she was saying.

'"The girl I left behind me," my lady.'

'Play something operatic and dignified,' said her ladyship. 'I will not have any cats'-meat tunes played by the band of the 21st Dragoon Guards.'

Outside the barrack-gates hundreds of people had assembled, mostly the wives and children of the troopers, bewailing the loss of their relatives, for only a few married women were allowed to accompany the regiment.

'If we were going to India they could not make more fuss,' said Lady Mulligan contemptuously.

As the regiment proceeded along the streets of London to the martial music, the cheering from the assembled crowds was tremendous. Mr. Cumbermore was riding in Hyde Park at the time. He rode up to Sir Titus, and had a few minutes' conversation with him. The hurrahs of the bystanders were redoubled in vigour. To the British public it seemed as if the young Prime Minister had at last shaken himself free of the 'Peace-at-any-price' party, and that he was really going to put his foot down, and settle the Irish question with the sword. The feeling against Ireland was intense in the Metropolis. One of the first things the Irish had done when Local Self-Government had been conceded to them some years before, was to put heavy duties on manufactures and all articles of commerce coming from England.

The English manufacturers and artisans who were for taxing foreign goods imported into England were indignant with the Irish for carrying out the same policy with reference to their own affairs. Nothing makes a peaceful Briton so irritable as to hit him in his pocket. The result was that the masses, which were previously indifferent to the murder of Loyalists in Ireland, and who had made more fuss about an elephant which was taken from London to the United States than about the mutilation of human beings on the other side of St. George's Channel, were now furious with the Irish people.

Indeed, Mr. Cumbermore himself had stated that it would be an easy matter to get up an anti-Irish movement throughout England, and have Irishmen expelled from England, as the Jews were expelled from Russia.

'Is it true, Mr. Cumbermore,' said Sir Richard Digby to that gentleman, who had joined the Baronet on leaving Sir Titus—'Is it true that you may safely appeal to the passions and prejudices of Englishmen but never to their reason?'

'It would indeed appear so very often,' said Mr. Cumbermore. 'Public opinion is, I fear, easily manufactured in this country. Just as the average juryman is first led one way by the counsel against the prisoner, then another by the delinquent's advocate, and finally gives his verdict upon the judge's remarks, so are the electors of Great Britain led by the nose. Some have a fetish they call Radicalism, others Toryism. It would puzzle them sorely to give the reasons for their political faith. As for the remainder, they are in a ship without rudder or compass, at the mercy of every political gust of wind.'

The troops arrived at the docks in time. The confusion at the barracks was nothing as compared with that which occurred at the place of embarkation. Women were trying to smuggle themselves on board to go with their husbands; horses were kicking violently as they were lowered into the vessel; officers and men were making desperate efforts to discover their respective berths; sailors were storing their ammunition; friends of the officers, who had been admitted on board, were continually getting in the way of the crew, and adding thus to the general confusion. Amongst the last to arrive was Mrs. Bruce, with Eugene. Tired and thoroughly worn out, she was in the act of going on board, when a young man accosted her, and informing her that he was one of the crew, offered to assist in finding out what accommodation there was for her.

'No, thank you,' she answered. 'Wait a moment, Eugene,' she added, addressing the boy.

'Eugene!' murmured the young man; 'this must be the boy.'

The speaker was Maggie, who was on the vessel, endeavouring to carry out some orders received from Barry.

Mrs. Bruce, who had been away for a minute to make some necessary inquiries, now returned, and led Eugene away.

Amongst a group of men on the steerage side of the vessel was the Fenian mulatto. He did not recognise Maggie as she passed him in her disguise. She trod, however, rather heavily on the cook's foot, who, in return, swore violently. In doing so, he remembered that it was connected with a preconcerted signal. When the deck was a little clear, the mulatto joined Maggie.

'Have you it here?' he said.

'Yes, everything is in the basket,' answered Maggie. 'Now show me the kitchen.'

'You look innocent enough in that garb,' said the mulatto with a grin, as he led the way down the steps.

CHAPTER XI.

AN unlooked-for incident occurred on board the *City of Rome* before the departure of the troops. Officers and men had succeeded in having their horses properly accommodated, and were lounging about the deck in small groups. Lady Mulligan was in a fury at the limited size of the cabin that had been provided for her; and her husband, finding himself in the way, was glad to escape on deck. Just as he reached the top of the cabin steps, he started back as if he had seen an apparition.

'Captain Belper—you here!' he exclaimed.

'Yes,' said Belper. 'I know I have disobeyed the Doctor's orders, but I could not let the ship sail without me. So here I am.'

'A gross piece of insubordination, sir!' said Sir Titus fiercely. 'If I did my duty I should place you under arrest.'

With these words Sir Titus strode towards a group of officers, frowning ominously. They dispersed to carry out some orders he gave, with no very good grace.

'What a bore old Titus is!' said Ostend to Digby as he and his companion walked away. 'He has just been giving it to poor Belper, simply because he disobeyed his doctor to be with his regiment.'

'What, is Arthur on board?' said Digby, with surprise. 'I had no idea of it. Where is his cabin?'

'He is sharing mine,' answered Ostend.

'I will show you the way.' And the Captain descended the stairs leading to the officers' quarters. They found Belper lying on his berth. He was very pale, and rose with difficulty to greet his comrades.

'It is too bad of you, my dear Arthur,' said Sir Richard. 'Titus is a brute, we all know; but it is really very rash of you to risk your life in this way.'

'I shall be better presently,' replied Arthur, who was looking very pale. 'I did not expect such a warm reception, and I am still weak.'

A knock came at the door.

'Come in,' said Captain Ostend, and Eugene answered to the summons.

Arthur's face brightened up as he saw the lad.

'Well, Eugene, how do you like being on board?' he said kindly.

'Very much, now you have come, sir,' answered the lad.

Eugene had brought some hot water in a can, which Belper tried to lift, but the effort was too great, and he was obliged reluctantly to abandon the idea.

'You are still weak, Arthur,' said Sir Richard, 'and I shall be your nurse. Let me have your berth, Ostend, and you take mine. I have a cabin to myself.'

Ostend readily assented, and left his two friends together, to seek his new quarters. The vessel by this time had weighed anchor. A thick mist covered the waters, and the lights of the passing boats could hardly be seen in the dense fog. All was still on the vessel, nothing being heard but the throbbing of the machinery, or the voices of the men on watch. Hard by the engine-room two men were busily engaged in placing some plates and dishes in a cupboard. From time to time they ceased working, and conversed together in a low tone of voice.

'See, it looks like a piece of coal,' said the taller of the two, who was Maggie, the Fenian agent. 'Only an experienced eye could distinguish the difference.'

'There is one thing I do not see,' said the mulatto, her companion. 'You are going to destroy the ship, but how are we to escape?'

'Very easily,' replied the woman; 'but you are in a great fright about your precious life. You ought to be proud to die for Ireland.'

'What is Ireland to me?' said the mulatto fiercely. 'I gain nothing by all this.'

'But you have a great deal to lose,' replied Maggie sharply. 'Your life, if you disobey my orders.'

The mulatto put on a resigned look, but his eyes glistened as he saw a cleaver lying on the table by his side.

'I know what is passing through your mind,' said Maggie, smiling. 'You are thinking how easy it would be to murder me. It would not benefit you. Within twenty-four hours you must die.'

'What do you mean?' asked the black, terror-stricken.

'I gave you a poison with your dinner,' answered the woman, 'knowing you were a traitor. To that poison there is but one antidote, and that is in my possession; but not on my person,' she added with a smile. 'You cannot fight against us, you see—we are too strong for you. Here, I have some more of the poison. Would you like to see how the drug does its deadly work?'

There was a fowl in a coop hanging

against the ship's side. The woman took the bird, and, squeezing its neck, put some of the poison down its throat.

'Watch the bird carefully,' she said, replacing the cage against the wall ; 'in two hours the bird will be dead ; but in far less time you will realize from its condition the tortures you will undergo. The antidote I shall not give you till after the explosion. I am now going to sleep.'

Curling herself up on a mattress in one corner, the Fenian emissary was soon buried in the most profound repose.

The mulatto, however, tried in vain to sleep. From time to time he looked anxiously at the bird, and then at the sleeper, wondering in his mind whether she had lied to him to terrify him into compliance with her designs. It was a long time to wait in such fearful suspense.

'If I were only sure,' he murmured, 'I would betray the plot to the captain.'

He arose at last from the ground with this determination, when a slight scratching sound reached his ear. He turned his head towards the direction from whence it came. The bird was pecking violently at the bars of its cage. He went up to it. The hen was evidently in great pain. Not content with pecking at the framework, she was driving her talons deep into her flesh, and scattering her feathers in the act. Between each convulsion there would be but an interval of one minute. He could not remain looking at the fearful sight alone, so he went to the sleeper, and shook her.

She smiled with satisfaction when she realized how completely she had the mulatto in her power.

The bird was now unable to stand. The

sounds became each moment fainter as she tried to reach the cage bars with her claws. Struggling from her recumbent position, she appeared for an instant, as it were, galvanized into life; then, fluttering her wings, she fell an inert mass on the floor of her prison.

The mulatto looked as terrified as if he had been viewing his own death-struggles.

'You have the antidote?' he gasped.

'I will give it you five minutes after the explosion takes place. The means for our escape are ready. Can you swim?'

'No.'

'It will not be necessary,' she replied carelessly. 'Here, in this bag, are two waterproof suits. After putting one of them on, all you have to do is to blow into the lining through an indiarubber funnel. The space below the outer and inner cloth becomes filled with air. You can float till doomsday. If you can, take a small paddle from the ship. The explosion will occur about twelve miles from the coast. It will be your own fault if you do not succeed in reaching the shore.'

'How shall we get into the sea without being detected?'

'Through the porthole by a rope,' answered Maggie. 'If you have any difficulty in getting through with your dress inflated, you must not blow into it till you are on the rope itself.'

Maggie went to the side of the ship, and looked out into the night.

'There is no moon,' she said; 'the fates mean to favour us.'

CHAPTER XII.

BLANCHE TRYINGTON was not at all sorry to hear that her aunt had determined to take her cousin and herself to the Mediterranean. She had been very ill since the day at Hurlingham when she had witnessed Captain Belper's accident. Often, as she sat in her boudoir at Arlington Street, had she catechized herself about the events of that day and the effect they had produced on her.

Had she really a tender interest in the welfare of Captain Belper? or was it merely the effect produced upon her nerves by seeing a fellow-creature in such imminent peril? Did she love Arthur Belper? She admired him, it was true. He was handsome, and brave, and truth was stamped upon his brow. She liked his society, she respected his qualities; but between these sentiments and love—the love that a noble woman should have for her future husband—there was a great, though apparently only a passable gulf.

Who was to define love to her? Who could open a heart, of which she only possessed the key? Was she piqued, as women sometimes are, at the mere resolution of a man to defy the boy Cupid? She argued these and many other ideas in her mind, but could arrive at no satisfactory conclusion.

Even supposing that she instinctively felt there was no other man who could rouse such feelings in her breast as the young officer, what right had she to encourage them, seeing that he had never shown the slightest predilection for her society in preference to that of any other person? He had chanced on one or two occasions to meet her at balls and dinners, and had ridden by her side in the Park, and at such times had made himself more than agreeable, even to the saying of pretty sentences; but who of her acquaintance had not done the same? However, in spite of all these things, he was ever in her thoughts, and she was loth to put those thoughts away from her mind. But now she was going to visit new countries, and would be free for a time from all the restraints of society. There would be no at homes, no calls to make, no teas, no dinners, no balls; and would she not be better able, out on the great blue Mediterranean, to put him out of her mind altogether? Alas, she felt there was no sea that could divide her from him in thought, no distance so great that it could divide her from him in spirit!

It was with a feeling of satisfaction, however, that she found herself with her aunt and cousin in a railway carriage on the way to Milford Haven. There they had arranged to meet Sir Richard Digby's yacht, and embark for Cadiz, Seville, and Gibraltar. Laura was by no means in a good humour at having to leave London before the expiration of the season. She had at last an object in life. Until now everything had bored her; but at last she had discovered some interest in existence, and that interest was centred in an object, and that object was to bring Arthur Belper to her knees. Not that she bore any affection for him, but merely because it amused her to do so, and, moreover, because she was determined that he should never marry her cousin Blanche.

And again, her views upon matrimony were not of a very elevated order, though they may have been orthodox, and she considered Captain Belper a very fair matrimonial speculation. He was of a good family, and had at least £7,000 a year; with only one drawback, the fact that he had no title to confer upon his wife. She had not closed her eyes to the state of her cousin's mind; and if she were able to achieve her purpose, she would by that means strike a mortal blow at Blanche's happiness. Laura hated her cousin. Lady Tryington she knew would leave half her fortune to Blanche, and that would leave her a very inadequate sum with which to supply her extravagant demands. She was quite unaware of the fact that Belper was about to embark for

Ireland, and was still under the impression that he was confined to his room. She had looked forward to meeting him in the Park on his recovery, and had exercised her brains not a little in devising new schemes with which to succeed in captivating the heart of the young dragoon. But now she was dragged away from the scene of her possible triumphs, to gratify the whims of Lady Tryington and the fads of her niece.

'Who ever heard of going to the Mediterranean in summer?' she had said, on hearing of the proposed voyage; 'it would ruin the complexion of a negress.'

Their journey so far at an end, the ladies found themselves at a comfortable hotel called 'The Dorking.' The best apartments had been prepared for them, and a special waiter hired for the occasion. In the landlord's opinion Lady Tryington was, to use his own expression, 'the nobbiest among the nobs,' and her visit to his hotel was an excellent advertisement for him. A waiter entered the room with a card upon a tray. 'Mr. Walsh' was written upon it, and underneath 'The *White Camellia*,' that being the name of Sir Richard Digby's yacht.

'Mr. Walsh,' said Lady Tryington; 'that is the name of Dick's captain.'

The captain of the *White Camellia* was announced. After receiving her ladyship's instructions, he withdrew to make the necessary arrangements for their reception on board the following day. The following morning broke cold and windy, but Lady Tryington was a woman of her word, and at five o'clock they were all on board the *White Camellia*.

The vessel had been newly fitted up by Sir Richard Digby's orders, and no expense had been spared to make the ladies' cabins as luxurious and comfortable as possible. Flowers were placed everywhere in abundance and with great taste, and an Erard's piano, with a quantity of new music, was a conspicuous feature in the saloon.

'How very thoughtful of Dick!' said Lady Tryington with real pleasure, as they walked through the ship.

'When would your ladyship like to sail?' said the captain, approaching them as they were curiously looking into the hold of the ship.

'As soon as possible, please,' was the answer.

'The barometer is falling very fast, my lady.'

'Never mind; we may as well get out to sea,' answered Lady Tryington.

Sir Richard Digby had given strict

orders that Lady Tryington's wishes were to be carried out in every respect. Walsh consequently did not think of suggesting that it might be advisable to postpone the departure. An excellent dinner had been prepared on board, and shortly after their repast the ladies retired to their cabins for the night. Very early the following morning they were awakened by the sound of sailors running about on deck.

The anchor was being weighed. An hour or two afterwards the vessel began to roll heavily.

'I thought we should catch it as soon as we got outside,' murmured Walsh to himself. 'The barometer falls steadily.'

Sir Richard Digby had engaged an experienced woman for the cruise in the person of a Mrs. Blenkinsop. She had crossed the Atlantic many times on board one of the vessels of the Cunard line, and had experienced all weathers.

'We are having a very bad passage, but it will be smoother presently,' said the worthy stewardess, tapping at Lady Tryington's cabin-door.

'We are caught in a gale, my lady,' she continued, as she received no answer; 'but you need not be alarmed.'

The position of the yacht was more perilous than even Mrs. Blenkinsop imagined; but she was under good hands, and all that could be done was being done. The captain had shortened sail; but the vessel, with almost bare masts, was scudding along at a great speed, driven by the wind and waves. An hour or more was passed in this predicament. To put into port was out of the question, the elements being too powerful. The only one who had thoroughly preserved her self-possession was the invalid, Blanche. Laura and Lady Tryington were confirmed in the opinion that their last hour had come. Lady Tryington slept after a while for some hours. When she awoke, there was no longer any need for anxiety—the wind had fallen. On deck, Captain Walsh was busily engaged in endeavouring to discover the damage his craft had received during the storm. She had shipped a quantity of water; but after a careful inspection the skipper came to the conclusion that there was no important leakage. However, several masts had been destroyed, and the vessel had been severely strained. It was absolutely necessary to put into some port for repairs. The yacht had been driven out of her course, and it would be necessary, before proceeding, to rest for a few days, while she was being refitted.

The sun was shining brightly in the

heavens. There was hardly a ripple on the waters. Mrs. Blenkinsop had assured the ladies that now all danger was at an end. Lady Tryington and her nieces were persuaded to come on deck, and having seated themselves beneath an awning, were watching the exertions of the crew, who were working with indefatigable energy. In the distance, a noble-looking steamer could be seen ploughing her way through the sunlit waters. Blanche was looking at this vessel with a field-glass which the captain had lent to her.

'She does not seem to have suffered so much as our yacht in last night's gale.'

As she said this, she turned to gaze in another direction. An exclamation from her cousin attracted her attention. A strange commotion appeared in the steamer. She seemed to have been suddenly upheaved, as if by a submarine convulsion.

Her masts were reeling over in the air. Detached portions of the vessel seemed to be floating about at a distance from it. A blue and vaporous smoke was rising from the waves. Suddenly, Captain Walsh was heard giving orders for the boats to be lowered. The sailors exercised every effort to get the boats into working order, and in ten minutes they were leaving the yacht for the wreck. In a moment, the sinking ship disappeared beneath the waves, never to rise again. It was a race for life, and the sailors strained every nerve to reach the scene of the disaster in time to save their fellow-creatures. From the deck of the *White Camellia* Blanche could see the figures of several people holding convulsively to the spars and fragments of the wreck. The sailors, though worn out with the fatigues of the previous night, still worked with a will, and with a determination worthy of the occasion. Laura had procured a large telescope from Sir Richard Digby's cabin, and the captain had fitted it up for her on a stand. Through the powerful lenses, the goal towards which the sailors were rowing could be distinctly seen. A spar had floated to a considerable distance from the other *débris*, and two people were holding on to this piece. In the meantime, Lady Tryington and Blanche had descended to the cabins to arrange for the reception of the survivors. Mrs. Blenkinsop was carrying out their instructions with great alacrity. The sailors were now rapidly approaching the immediate scene of the disaster.

'Steady all!' shouted the man in command of the first boat. 'I see two figures moving on our right.'

A voice was heard calling for assistance. A few minutes afterwards two men were hoisted into the boat; one was dead, the other insensible. The boat was rowed forward. At a short distance, some more of the steamer's passengers were found, and were at once removed from the planks to which they were clinging. Three persons could be seen close at hand—one of them being a woman—and they were soon safe on board. In an hour, or a little more, the yacht's boat was turning away from the catastrophe, and making towards the *White Camellia,* with many survivors in the little craft. Hardy, the man in command, had heard that the lost steamer was called the *City of Rome.* As the boat reached the yacht, Lady Tryington and her nieces were anxiously counting the number of people saved from the wreck. Alas! only seven had been rescued alive. An exclamation from Blanche, who had turned suddenly pale, attracted Lady Tryington's attention.

'What is it, my child?' she said anxiously.

'Oh, aunt!' exclaimed her niece. 'Look, look! there is Dick, and Captain Belper; what—what does it mean? Oh! I must be dreaming.'

Blanche was not dreaming. There, true enough, was Sir Richard Digby, supporting Belper on his arm, and seated near to them were Mrs. Bruce and Eugene. The poor woman was in tears, for her husband had been lost in the wreck. She had only been saved herself by the presence of mind displayed by Eugene, who immediately the explosion took place had seized two lifebelts, one of which he had given to the woman. Sir Richard Digby had only been able to find one, and that he had placed round Belper, trusting himself to his strong arms for safety.

A few hours afterwards, Sir Richard

was sitting at dinner with his aunt and her nieces, giving them a detailed account of their misfortunes on board the *City of Rome.*

'But how did it occur?' said Blanche eagerly.

'We have that to learn yet,' answered Digby. 'My impression was that a boiler had burst, but the explosion did not seem to me to have happened in that part of the ship. The moment it occurred, however, in poured the water to such an extent that it was immediately seen the pumps were useless. All the soldiers were on deck. By the Colonel's orders we called the roll. While that was being done, the captain of the ship said, in an undertone, that the life boats had been destroyed.

'"Attention!" shouted the Colonel.

'You could have heard a pin drop, but for the rushing of the water into the ship.

'"Men of the 21st," said Sir Titus Mulligan, "our ship is going down. Die like men. Save the women if you can. If there be a survivor, let him be able to say that the 21st looked death in the face as readily as they have done a hundred times before."

'One cheer rose from the ranks as the Colonel finished speaking. It sounded like a requiem over the dying.

'I cannot describe the confusion which ensued. Women rushing hither and thither in search of their husbands, willing to die only in their arms. Lady Mulligan was as calm and collected as her husband. The waters were now surrounding us, and I remember very little more with any certainty, till I found myself in the waves, surrounded by hundreds struggling with death, from which so few of the brave fellows escaped.'

Sir Richard Digby drank a glass of wine to cover his emotion as he finished speaking.

The survivors had been quartered in the cabins, and every attention was being paid to their wants.

Blanche remembered that night to pour out her heart in gratitude to Him who holds the waters in the hollow of His hand for the souls who had been saved that day from the wreck. Creeping quietly up on deck, after the others had retired for the night, she leaned over the side of the vessel, and looked out into the night. The moon was riding calmly over the peaceful waters, and casting its reflection on the dark blue waves.

A figure passed slowly near her in the darkness, and descended the cabin steps. By the light of the moon she discerned the face and form of Arthur Belper. In his hand he held a rose, which he placed lightly and reverentially to his lips. It was the one she had given him at Hurlingham. He paused a moment before descending the steps, and placed his fingers delicately amongst the faded petals.

'She gave me a rose,' he said softly to himself. 'Will she ever give me a still more precious gift?'

CHAPTER XIII.

MAGGIE was one of the survivors. The explosion had taken place long before the hour upon which she had calculated. She had seen the horrors worked by her own remorseless hand, and such an effect had it produced on her mind that she would gladly have shared the fate of those who had been drowned.

Arthur Belper suffered from a great depression, which lasted some days. He could scarcely realize that his brother officers, the men with whom he had passed so many happy years, had gone from his sight for ever.

The remembrance of the scene on deck, too, preyed upon his mind, and rendered him prostrate and delirious.

Blanche slept very little on the night following the day of the disaster. The horrors of the shipwreck were too vividly imprinted on her mind. But with it all, she was more grateful than words could express that Arthur Belper had been saved. She had heard, too, his avowal of love to the poor rose she had given him at Hurlingham, and she could no longer blind herself to the fact that his love was fully reciprocated by her.

Laura had not given a second thought to the unfortunate crew of the *City of Rome*. She only realized that once more Arthur Belper was near her, and in a position where she would have every opportunity of exercising all her powers of fascination.

On the following morning, Digby, who was the first to appear on deck, found Walsh busily engaged in superintending some repairs to the vessel.

'We had better put in at Holyhead, and have her refitted there,' said the skipper to his master.

This seemed the wisest course to pursue, and Sir Richard gave instructions accordingly. It was necessary, moreover, that he and Arthur Belper should present themselves to the authorities as soon as possible. They would both be required as witnesses before the Court of Inquiry which would be certain to be assembled to investigate the cause of the loss of the vessel. Again, they could the sooner be attached to some other regiment, for affairs in Ireland were very critical, and the Baronet was aware that the arrival of the American contingent in Ireland was the prelude to a life-and-death struggle between the Celts and Saxons.

Whilst conversing with the skipper, the three ladies came on deck, accompanied by Captain Belper. He was still very ill and weak, and after some persuasion he was induced to return to the saloon and recline upon a sofa.

Blanche looked anxiously at Sir Richard Digby as he returned from accompanying him.

'I wish,' said Digby, as if in answer to her mute appeal—'I wish, Blanche, you and Laura would see that he is properly looked after, for he requires great care.'

Maggie had been watching this scene from a distance, and she fully realized its meaning. Nothing escaped her keen eye—not even the anxious expression on Blanche's face as she watched Arthur being led away. From the captain she had gathered that Belper and Sir Richard Digby were great friends. It gradually dawned on her recollection that Belper was the one who had saved Eugene's life. Then there was something in Sir Richard Digby's face that was not unfamiliar to her. It haunted her continually, but she could not recall under what circumstances she had seen it before, for it to have so clearly impressed itself on her memory.

She ran back over the years of her past life. Oh, those years! what would she not give to recall and re-spend them! Then she thought of Eugene, with his fair, handsome, and open face, and a shade of regret passed over her countenance as she thought how little the love of any human being had ever entered into her life.

She paced the deck moodily, thinking of those on board the *White Camellia*, and of the face of Sir Richard Digby, whom she felt sure she had seen before.

'Where have I met him?' she said fretfully in her thoughts. 'Where have I met him? If I could only pick up the links, what a chain I might forge!'

CHAPTER XIV.

'A CABINET COUNCIL IN DOWNING STREET.
THE "CITY OF ROME" GONE DOWN IN THE BRITISH CHANNEL—ALL HANDS LOST.
GREAT BATTLE NEAR DUBLIN—DEFEAT OF THE ENGLISH TROOPS.
FRESH RISING IN INDIA—MASSACRE OF ENGLISH NEAR DELHI.
DETERMINED ATTITUDE OF THE VOLUNTEERS.'

THIS was the alarming placard of a London journal, which caught the eye of the Fenian Barry as he was walking in one of his numerous disguises, through Piccadilly Circus, in the direction of the Strand, where he was going to attend a meeting of the conspirators.

'Good!' he said to himself, as he walked on; 'Maggie has done her work well. Now, if we can only destroy the Members of the Cabinet, we shall be one more step in the direction of Ireland's freedom.'

Immense excitement prevailed not only in the metropolis, but in every town and city throughout the kingdom. Meetings of the Volunteer forces, in defiance of the order of the Queen's regulations, had been held in many parts of England, to denounce the Peace-at-any-price party with reference to India and Ireland.

Lord Cromer, a distinguished general, who had been removed from the army on account of his political views by Mr. Cumbermore, presided at several of these meetings in the metropolis. It was rumoured that the Militia and Regulars would join with the Volunteers. Lord Cromer had publicly declared that under existing circumstances Parliamentary Government was a farce. The effigies of the Members of the Government had been burned in public thoroughfares, amid great cheering and rejoicing.

'A house divided against itself cannot stand long, but time is everything to our cause; for, let Cromer once establish a Military Government, the spirit of the country might assert itself, and all would be lost.'

Another plot had been formed, under Barry's superintendence, for the destruction of the Cabinet Ministers. It had been thought by the Fenian leader that, as so many attempts had been made on their lives and had been frustrated by Metrale, the Chief of the Police, now perhaps he might, buoyed up by success, have relaxed his vigilance.

Besides which, Barry had hit upon a

plan which he thought would completely baffle the police. The large cistern on the roof of the Foreign Office had been out of order for some time, but had recently been put into repair. The pipe for filling it with water was attached, but the cistern itself was empty. Barry received this information from a Fenian in his service, who had been employed as a plumber in the work. By means of a plan of the sewers and underground communications of London, in the conspirator's possession, he had ascertained the exact position of the pipe that supplied the Foreign Office with water. His men had taken a house, beneath which the pipe passed. They had orders at a certain time to tap it, and then, by means of a small but powerful steam-engine, to force petroleum into the cistern. It was further arranged that at a given signal the plumber, who had arranged to secrete himself on the roof, was to turn a tap which, for the extinction of fire at the Foreign Office, was connected with the reservoir on the roof. The building would at once become fairly saturated with petroleum, and, what with the fires and the gas burning below, it would be indeed strange if a single person within the walls were to escape the conflagration. Never had a more diabolical plan been formed; and it was to meet his associates, and discuss the final arrangements of the plot, that Barry, the arch-conspirator, was making his way when the placard struck his eye.

The rooms in the lower part of the Foreign Office were being painted and whitewashed, and this would cause the Members of the Cabinet to hold their council in one of the upper rooms.

On reaching Charing Cross, the conspirator entered a small, mean-looking house. It had formerly been a pawnbroker's shop, but the owner had become bankrupt, and had consequently to give up business. The house had then been advertised as to let, and Mike, Barry's lieutenant, had taken possession, paying down the first quarter's rent. It was now a common rendezvous for the Fenians, and as the cellars communicated with the sewers of London, they afforded a means of escape in the event of the house being surrounded by the police.

On entering the house, the chief conspirator walked rapidly to a small yard at the back of the premises, first carefully closing the door behind him. He had previously whistled in a low tone, and the signal had been answered in a similar manner. Once in the yard, he looked cautiously round, and then, perceiving that he was unobserved, removed a large bundle of faggots, when a trap-door was disclosed, evidently covering a well. It had been placed there previously, to prevent people from falling into the hole. A slight noise was heard at the bottom of the pit, and it was evident from the sound that the well was quite dry. Some object was gradually being pushed upwards, reaching in time the level of the ground, and remaining in that position. It was a ladder arranged on a telescopic system, and which drew out to any length required—a very convenient invention, as it could be elevated in a very confined space. Taking hold of the topmost rung, Barry lowered himself till he found a foothold, and in a few minutes he was at the bottom of the well, where his lieutenant was anxiously waiting his arrival.

'Is everything in preparation?' inquired the chief.

'Yes,' said Mike, 'our men are hard at work at the pump.' And stooping down, he crouched beneath a low arch into a narrow passage, which led to an opening in one of the main sewers. A footpath had been made beneath this huge drain. Along it Mike walked, bearing a lantern, and followed by his chief. After proceeding some few hundred yards the lieutenant stopped, and stooping once more, passed through another arch similar to the one by which he had entered the sewer. Barry now found himself in a large vault, presumably at one time a dungeon belonging to an old mansion that centuries before had been erected near the Thames. Several men were at work here, and in the middle of the cellar was a small, noiseless steam-engine. The gauge showed that this machine was working at high pressure.

'Just over our heads,' said Mike to

Barry, 'are the tanks belonging to Gilot and Son, the petroleum importers. They contain thousands of gallons of paraffin, and we have tapped them successfully, and they are now forcing the liquid through this pipe into the cistern above the Foreign Office.'

A red light from some torches that were burning in a corner of the chamber threw its lurid rays on the faces and forms of the Fenian conspirators, as, stripped to the waist, they were engaged—some in feeding the furnace, others in attaching a fresh pipe to the fierce little pumps of the engine.

Barry looked at his watch.

'It is now about five o'clock,' he remarked. 'Everything will be ready by seven, will it not?'

'As near as possible,' answered Mike.

'Mr. Cumbermore will not return from Windsor before night,' said the chief of the Fenians. 'A special train has been ordered to be in readiness at 7·30, to bring him to town. The Cabinet Council cannot be held before nine or half-past. So that we shall be in perfect readiness for the signals. By the way, have any of you heard or seen anything of Maggie? It is now three days since the explosion took place, and she ought to have been with us by this time, unless she paid with her life for her success.'

No one had heard of her, but all were anxious. Barry issued his final orders, and then retraced his steps to the mouth of the well. Leaving his lieutenant in the old house at Charing Cross, he went in search of some information about Maggie.

'I must keep my eye on her,' he said, as once more the newspaper boys thrust their papers before him. 'She is a desperate and successful ally, but she would be a dangerous foe.'

CHAPTER XV.

THE people of England were becoming very dissatisfied with the continual reverses experienced by their armies. Mr. Bullneck found it very difficult, in spite of his great oratorical powers, to induce English audiences to pass Peace-at-any-price resolutions. Indeed, some of his meetings had been disturbed of late by advocates of the Military Government, and the old agitator now saw that if he wished to go with the times, he would have not to agitate for a peace policy, but to outbid Cumbermore, and go in for upholding what the military element throughout the kingdom were pleased to call the honour of Old England.

Lord Cromer had been very active in arousing his fellow-countrymen from their lethargy to denounce the principles upheld by Mr. Cumbermore, and also the degrading tenets of Mr. Bullneck's policy. Many who before had been antagonistic to these ideas were now won over to their opponents by the stagnation of trade. Factories were lying idle, and men thrown out of work. Whole towns had become depopulated, and thousands of men and women, who formerly had earned an honest livelihood, were now obliged to leave their native country and emigrate with their children to foreign lands.

The result had been a complete revulsion of feeling in many of the constituencies. The Scotch alone were still somewhat Radical, but through the reverses of British troops, and the knowledge that their own country might even be invaded by a mixed force of Celts and Americans, they were becoming reconciled to the idea that perhaps a military dictatorship for the time would be the best form of Government.

Stringent orders had been sent from the War Office to Lord Cromer, to the effect that he must desist from delivering public speeches against the Government. The Volunteers had been warned that unless they put an end to their unlawful meetings they would be disbanded. But Lord Cromer, whose name had some years previously been erased from the 'Army List' at the instigation of Mr. Cumbermore, treated these mandates with contempt; and the Volunteers, instead of being awed by the communications they had received, showed their indifference to the threats by increasing the number of their gatherings. Lord Cromer was in confidential correspondence with officers commanding other Volunteer corps throughout the kingdom. He was known as a good general, and a determined, high-minded man. Many officers had agreed to obey him implicitly whenever he gave the order for an outbreak, and the Metropolitan Volunteers to a man were believed to be on his side. Information as to the probable extent of this conspiracy had been already forwarded by Metrale to the Prime Minister. Indeed, the Cabinet Council to be held in Downing Street related to that very subject. Members of Parliament, who had voted at unsettled times for the surrender by England of her various colonies, had been hissed on their way to Westminster by a mob representing not only the lower, but all classes of society; and Mr. Bullneck, the leader of the extreme party, had been stoned on two occasions, and his life placed in peril.

Under the circumstances, it seemed strange that Mr. Cumbermore did not meet the threatening storm by an appeal to the country. But he was a determined man, and an able though unscrupulous statesman. His love of power and office was unbridled. His good opinion of himself at all times made him overbearing and despotic, and to see his foes, the Imperialists—whom he had contemptuously denounced as Jingoes—in office would have been too much for him to endure.

He had sent almost every available soldier belonging to the regular army to Ireland, and was in hopes that the next telegram would bring him news of the suppression of the insurrection. Should this have taken place he could then appeal to the country ; but not under existing circumstances, as a dissolution would be fatal to the Radical Party, of which he had been so long the leader. He was now with the Sovereign at Windsor, having been summoned there on account of the alarming reports which had reached the Court as to the reverses experienced by British troops in Ireland, and the unsettled state of the country owing to the Fenian outrages. It had been publicly stated in Parliament by the Secretary of State for War that the reports had been much exaggerated, but the fact remained that the telegraph wires had been cut, and that there was no communication with Dublin for the time being. The Court had been further alarmed by a report that the Household Troops and the Foot Guards, upon whom the Sovereign could rely implicitly, had been disbanded owing to their monarchical tendencies, and that their barracks had been filled by the Metropolitan Police.

The news from India, too, was of an alarming nature. The Commander-in-Chief of the Forces in Hindostan had telegraphed that without reinforcements it would be impossible to subdue the insurgents ; that the Afghans had crossed the Indus ; and that, bad as had been the state of things in India at the time of the Sepoy rebellion, it was now a great deal worse. The fact was that Mr. Cumbermore's policy had been to educate the natives of Hindostan, under the impression that if they were well instructed they would see how much more beneficial it would be for them to be under British rule than under the dominion of Russia. He had not taken into his consideration that on learning their own strength they might wish to govern themselves. Since the Indians had been taught to read English in the native schools, the sale of newspapers published in Ireland had increased enormously in the large towns throughout Hindostan. It was known that Irishmen had obtained Home Rule by means of outrages and murders, and this knowledge had induced the natives of Hindostan to try the same argument with a like object in their own case.

The Sovereign's hand was extended to Mr. Cumbermore as he entered the private apartments. The Prime Minister kissed it, but with a somewhat contemptuous air, as if in his opinion it was time that such a ceremony should be dispensed with.

'Any fresh news from Ireland, Mr. Cumbermore?'

'No, your Majesty; but I am hourly expecting to hear that the insurrection has been suppressed, and that the rebel leaders are prisoners in the hands of the authorities.'

'And from Hindostan what tidings have you?'

'Alas! nothing of an encouraging nature,' replied Mr. Cumbermore. 'The Commander-in-Chief telegraphs that he requires more troops, and we have none to send.'

'But the reserves; surely they might be employed. They were called out some weeks ago, if my memory serves me.'

'Impossible for us to let them leave England, your Majesty. We are daily in dread of a rising against your Majesty's Government. The Volunteers and Militia are quite prepared to make a movement under Lord Cromer.'

'The country is in a very disturbed condition,' observed the Sovereign. 'The feeling against my advisers seems to be very strong.'

As the Monarch spoke, a page entered the room with a despatch. It was directed to the Prime Minister, and on it was written ' Urgent.'

' By your Majesty's permission ?' said Mr. Cumbermore inquiringly.

On reading the first few lines, Mr. Cumbermore's countenance betrayed considerable agitation of mind. The letter was from Lord O'Hagan Harton. It ran as follows :

' Metrale's information from private sources leads me to believe that the rebels have taken Dublin. The news is not yet public, and I have given orders that it be suppressed. This, however, can only last a day or two, as the people must learn the truth in time. Our military advisers say the tunnel ought to be destroyed as soon as the troops have returned. Cromer has made another revolutionary speech to-day. Don't fail to be at the Cabinet meeting this evening.'

Mr. Cumbermore was obliged to inform the Sovereign of the contents of the despatch, and he remained another half-hour in the Monarch's presence, after which he was conducted in one of the Royal carriages to the station.

How different was his reception by the spectators on that occasion to that which in former times he had received! There was no demonstration, although it was known that the Prime Minister would leave Windsor at a certain hour.

Mr. Ryder happened to be returning to London by the same train, with the intention of gleaning sufficient information for a paragraph in the *Scrawler*, but he found the Prime Minister gloomy and uncommunicative.

Half an hour after their departure the train steamed into Paddington Station, and Lord O'Hagan Harton was anxiously awaiting the arrival of his colleague.

'The Duke of Preston will meet you to-night,' said the Lord Chancellor, as they drove off in his carriage. 'He is an authority on Indian matters.'

'It will be interesting to hear his views,' said the Prime Minister. 'I should like to see him before the meeting to-night.'

'Cromer is getting a dangerous foe,' said Lord O'Hagan Harton.

'Yes; the matter must come before the council to-night. He is a man of action, not words only. He remembers that I was the means of having his name erased from the "Army List," and if the opportunity were afforded him, he would strike deeply. We must arrest Lord Cromer for high treason. The difficulty will be to take him. Metrale can depend thoroughly on some of the men in his force. They will go to Cromer's residence at night, dressed in Volunteer uniform. A special train will be in waiting to convey him to London. If it is properly carried out, his men will be ignorant of the capture.'

'It would go hard with the policemen if they were discovered,' answered his colleague. 'The papers say he has 40,000 men at his back, with the pretence of manœuvring under his command. What terrible days we live in! Who would have thought that under a free and enlightened Radical Government England would be on the eve of a revolution?'

'Yes,' replied the Prime Minister; 'and what perplexes me is that the movement is not against the Crown—I wish it were—but against ourselves; against us, who have enfranchised the lower classes because we thought it would keep us in office—who have given up the colonies because we thought it would be economical to do so—who sold Gibraltar to the Spaniards, and were able in consequence to abolish the income tax ; against us, who strive daily to do away with that costly appendage Royalty—who have abolished the Household Troops, nominally on the ground of expense—who gave the people caucuses to save them the trouble of even thinking for themselves: and it is against us that the popular feeling is directed. Truly, ingratitude so great is unparalleled in history.'

'But we must dine now,' said the Lord Chancellor, 'and drown our woes in a good glass of wine, and then go at once to the Cabinet meeting.'

'There to decide on the fall of Lord Cromer,' added the Prime Minister for the subject was uppermost in his mind.

CHAPTER XVI.

IT was a pleasant afternoon in the middle of the month of June, and the large town of Meltingborough presented an unusually animated appearance. On the following day it had been arranged that the great Volunteer review should take place. From all parts of the Midland counties, and in some instances from the North of the Tweed, Volunteers had arrived in their thousands and tens of thousands to be present on the occasion.

The country round Meltingborough was admirably suited for a military spectacle—large tracks of moorland spreading for miles in every direction, surrounded by a broken chain of hills—and afforded space for 200,000 men to march past if required to do so, and at the same time allowed the spectators to view the military movements from the adjoining hills, without hampering the manœuvres of the soldiers.

The rifle-butts of the Meltingborough Volunteers were celebrated throughout the kingdom, there being a sufficient range even for the manipulation of the new machine guns, which from their accuracy and rapidity of fire were revolutionizing the system of armament in the British army.

Lord Cromer's castle, a magnificent mansion, was in the vicinity of Meltingborough. The park had been thrown open to the Volunteers during their encampment, and long lines of tall tents studded the glades where a few days previous antlered monarchs had held undivided sway.

Lord Cromer had greatly distinguished himself in India, and could show the trace of many a wound received in a hard-won fight. On returning to England he became a legislator, and joined the Conservative Party, his powers of organization being of the greatest service to his leaders.

There was, perhaps, no man in England who was such a thorn in the side of the revolutionary party as Lord Cromer. Whenever the Radicals formed caucuses he would start rival caucuses; not that he approved of the mode of warfare, but because he thought it necessary to fight the revolutionists with their own weapons. When Mr. Cumbermore organized meetings where ten thousand people were brought together to listen to his eloquence —and he could talk—Lord Cromer would organize rival meetings where a still greater number of people were brought together to listen to himself. When Mr. Cumbermore's organ, the *Rattlesnake*, announced that gigantic meetings had been held in twenty large towns throughout the kingdom, Lord Cromer's organ, the *Sovereign and People*, declared that in forty centres of industry meetings had been held to express their sympathy with the policy of his party, and their disgust at the unpatriotic and degrading conduct of Mr. Cumbermore and his followers. Mr. Cumbermore, to secure a larger circulation of the *Rattlesnake*, reduced his paper from twopence to a penny, slightly diminishing the size of that journal; whereupon Lord Cromer increased the amount of matter in the *Sovereign and People* and sold it for a halfpenny. It was a case of diamond cut diamond, and war to the knife, between the two statesmen; and Lord Cromer waited calmly but hopefully for an opportunity to avenge himself upon the Prime Minister for having struck his name from the 'Army List' for what the Prime Minister chose to describe as 'a grave breach of discipline,' but which was really the result of Lord Cromer speaking his mind too freely against the Premier's method of promoting those only who swore political allegiance to him, and also on account of his writing to the press letters condemning this form of bribery, and branding it as unconstitutional and degrading.

Lord Cromer was now engaged in visiting the encampment of the Volunteers. The rumour of his arrival had spread rapidly along the lines of tents, and on all sides he was greeted with every show of affection and loyalty. He was a born leader of men, and his followers intuitively felt it, and would have followed him even in a forlorn hope. Several officers came forward and besought him to address the men.

'It is against orders,' said his lordship, with a faint smile. 'Do you think we are powerful enough with this army at our backs to make our own regulations?'

At that moment a murmur arose from all sides—a faint but perceptible murmur that sounded like an approaching storm.

'Speak, speak!' said the officers; 'the men will hear you.'

Lord Cromer turned his horse's head round towards the Castle, and, riding to a convenient elevation, held up his right hand.

By this time some 20,000 men had gathered round him, and a dead silence reigned as the popular General raised his hand. In a voice that would have encouraged the faintest heart amongst them, he addressed these words to the assembled multitude of armed men :

'Volunteers of England, you are assembled to-day nominally for the purpose of drill ; in reality, you are here as representatives of public opinion—that voice so powerful that it has been called the voice of God. The members of the Revolutionary Government have tried to stifle it, but in vain. Each day that these men are in power brings more humiliation upon England. Everywhere our arms are reversed, and our flag is trodden in the mire. The Prime Minister, who has been called upon to dissolve Parliament, refuses to do it, so lustful is he of office and power. He once said that force is no remedy. Are you prepared, Volunteers of England, to show him that it is a very powerful remedy ? If so, speak as one man, and to-morrow I will lead you to London.

Strike, Volunteers, for Old England and our Sovereign !'

A tremendous cheer arose from the assembled multitude as Lord Cromer finished speaking ; and, from the wild enthusiasm, it was evident that a spirit of determination had been communicated from the General to his men.

'The die is cast,' said Lord Cromer to himself, as he rode back from the camp, escorted by the commanding officers of the various battalions. 'The die is cast. Now, Cumbermore, look to yourself! One of us must fall.'

CHAPTER XVII.

IT was night in the old Castle of Meltingborough. A dinner had been given by its owner to the Volunteer officers, and over four hundred had assembled in the great hall of the Castle. It was a grand spectacle, and did honour even to the place which for generations had fostered sons whose lives had been ever at the service of their country. On this occasion a number of loyal toasts had been proposed. The Sovereign's health had been drunk with great enthusiasm. It was clear, from the applause with which Lord Cromer's remarks were received, that the Volunteers of England were united in their devotion to the Crown; and, by the observations that fell from the lips of some of the more influential, it was manifest that they were animated with a common feeling of bitter hatred towards the Government. It was whispered that, if Mr. Cumbermore only had their leaders in his power, their lives would be the forfeit of their present action. The rumour reached Lord Cromer's ears, and he took advantage of the opportunity afforded him to speak.

'Gentlemen,' he said, 'it may not have struck you as very remarkable that on this occasion the health of the Cabinet Ministers has been omitted on the list of toasts. I look upon them as traitors to their country, and I now ask you to drink with me to the dire punishment that awaits them.'

The remarks of Lord Cromer were received on every occasion with great enthusiasm; and, after arranging for an early parade of the whole force in the camp, Lord Cromer retired from the room, accompanied by two of his most trusted officers. They proceeded to his lordship's library, where arrangements were made for the movement of the soldiers to the Metropolis. Lord Cromer was well aware that Mr. Cumbermore by that time had received a report of his speech, and that in all probability an order would be issued for his arrest. Indeed, so concerned was one of his officers, Sir Edward Righton, at the risk his leader ran of being made a prisoner, that on his own responsibility he had thrown out a line of outposts around the Castle, with orders to detain anyone not in uniform approaching the walls of the building.

'There will be some difficulty in railway

transport,' observed Sir Edward Righton, 'although the stationmasters and the other officials are with us to a man ; but I have carried out your orders, and sent two companies, under Colonel Trent, to the stations, with orders to detain all trains and secure as many carriages as possible. At the same time, I have sent some men to cut the wires that connect us with London. It will not do for Cumbermore to be apprised sooner than need be of our intentions.'

'Unfortunately we have no artillery,' said Lord Cromer ; 'but it has its advantage, for we should have experienced great difficulty in transporting the guns. I propose that we move by rail to within about fifteen miles of London, and then dividing into several corps, at a given signal each commander will march from four different points of the compass on the

City. The Metropolitan Volunteers are with us to a man; and all the men Cumbermore can rely upon are the police—even they are wavering. As to the regular army, what regiments there are in London may be compelled to make an ineffectual stand; but it will be of short duration, and they will willingly surrender. Once the blow is struck, they will hail with equal delight the downfall of the Radical tyrants.'

A servant entered the room, with a card for Lord Cromer.

'The gentleman has been detained by Sir Horace Holcroft, my lord, awaiting your orders.'

'Just see who it is, Righton,' said Lord Cromer, who was too occupied with a map that was spread before him to look up.

'Sir Richard Digby.'

'Digby!' exclaimed his lordship. 'Digby,

my own nephew! Oh! this is fortunate indeed. Bring him here yourself, Righton. You remember the man who was in the 21st Dragoon Guards. He will be a useful man if we can enlist his sympathies. He knows his work well, and is a capital staff officer. Perhaps, on consideration, it would be better for me to meet him alone. Take him to the east room in the long gallery.'

Sir Edward Righton went upon his mission, and Lord Cromer turned to his other officer.

'Are we well supplied with ammunition?'

'Fully.'

'Remember, once we leave Meltingborough, where we can procure everything we want, it will be difficult to find the means of supplying cartridges for our machine guns and repeating rifles.'

'All this has been attended to,' said the officer.

'Then we move to London to-morrow.' And, saying good-night to his friend, Lord Cromer proceeded to the east room to meet his nephew.

'How altered you are, Dick!' said Lord Cromer, after a warm and hearty greeting. 'Let me see, how long is it since we last met? It must be ten years, if it is a day.'

'Yes, uncle; time does not make us any younger in appearance, if it cannot steal our boyish spirits.'

'But how did you come here?'

'I arrived at Meltingborough on my way to town this afternoon. In the railway station I heard of your speech to the Volunteers; and, as it appeared to me you meant business, I determined to offer my services.'

'What, against the Government?'

'Yes, heartily; they are going from bad to worse, and I shall be glad to assist in bringing them to their knees.'

They sat some time by the old oak fire-place, talking over old times and old campaigns; and Lord Cromer felt the old attachment for his nephew stronger than ever when they parted for a few hours' rest.

Rest, though, was out of the question for Lord Cromer. He sat himself down to study his maps, and to finish his plan for provisioning his army on the march. If Lord Cromer, as he sat in the old-fashioned library, had not been so engrossed in his occupation, he might have heard a slight noise as of something being placed against the wall outside his room. At the sound, several birds flew away from the ivy which clung to the walls. Two men, dressed in Volunteer uniform, were placing a short ladder against the masonry. Presently one of them ascended, and, looking carefully through the window of the room where his lordship was writing, made a sign to his companion, and then descended. For some time they both remained concealed in the shadows cast by the massive buttresses of the building. An hour passed, and again the man ascended the ladder, only to return to his companion again. Another hour passed, and once more the same man mounted the rungs of the ladder, and repeated the operation. This time Lord Cromer was no longer at work. Worn out by his mental and bodily exertions, he had fallen asleep on a couch. By the faint light of the lamp, the intruder could see the pallid countenance of the sleeper. Making a sign to his comrade below, the latter climbed to within a few feet of the window. Meantime his companion, taking out of his pocket a glazier's diamond, pressed it against one of the large panes of glass, at the same moment making a circular movement with his wrist. Then, taking a large piece of brown paper, he smeared it with some sticky substance, and placed it over the entire glass. Waiting patiently for a quarter of an hour, he then removed the paper, and found the piece of glass excised by the diamond adhering to the paper. All this had been effected without any noise, and even if Lord Cromer had been awake, his attention would hardly have been aroused by the proceedings. Putting his hand carefully through the hole in the glass, the man drew back the bolt that fastened the casement, pouring at the same time some oil into the chinks of the woodwork. The window opened without much effort, and with very little noise. Telling his companion to follow him, he stepped across the sill into the room. Not a sound could be heard save the deep breathing of Lord Cromer, who, with his face turned to the wall, and resting on his arm, lay buried in a profound sleep. The flickering lamp gave a ghastly appearance to the two men, as they crept stealthily to the table. The first one to enter the room whispered to his companion in a low tone, and by the gesticulations which accompanied his remarks, it was evident that it was a mooted point in the speaker's mind as to whether it would not be the wisest thing to kill the sleeper, and then to escape as fast as possible.

The other, however, dissuaded his companion from this course of action.

'The chief does not want him to be killed,' said the man.

A look of incredulity passed over the first speaker's face.

'Perhaps not. He wants him to be a prisoner in his hands; but if he wakes, we have no other course.'

Turning the wick of the lamp a little higher, the speaker took from his pocket a small bottle, and, after extracting the cork, poured the contents on some wool. A powerful and sickly odour pervaded the atmosphere as the wool was saturated by the liquid; and having placed it on the pillow, the man retreated behind a curtain, whither his companion had already secreted himself, to wait for the poisoned air to take effect on the sleeper. In a few minutes the sound of heavy breathing, which before had filled the room, died gradually away, each moment becoming more intermittent and less audible, and ceasing altogether at last.

'So far we are successful,' said the man who had administered the anæsthetic, 'but we cannot administer chloroform to him all the way up to town; a little of the extract of morphia will do our business better.'

With these words, he took from a small leather case a little instrument, and inserting it into the sleeper's arm, injected something beneath his skin.

'He will be quiet now for at least forty-eight hours,' said the operator; 'indeed, if he is not a strong man, he will sleep till Doomsday.'

'Now let us put on his uniform,' said the other.

Raising the body of the peer, with the assistance of his accomplice, he slowly dressed his victim, buckling on the sword-belt, and putting the cocked-hat on the General's head.

'He looks quite life-like,' said the man, with a smile of satisfaction.

'Yes; if it were daytime, we should have all the Guards turning out to salute his lordship,' said the other, with a grin.

'As it is,' continued the other, 'he will not be recognised; and even if that were to happen, they will think he is going to inspect the pickets. The special train is waiting at a little station seven miles distant, and if we can once clear the lines, there will be little difficulty in finishing our work.'

Raising Lord Cromer in their arms, they carried him to the window, and, strapping a broad leather belt around his waist, they attached it to a long cord with knots at intervals of one or two feet to prevent its slipping. Placing their victim on the top of the ladder, they allowed him to slide quietly down the incline.

A few minutes afterwards they might have been seen driving down the park avenue which led to the main road.

CHAPTER XVIII.

IT was about two hours before dawn, just the time that a general with his wits about him generally selects to attack the camp of the enemy. Sir Richard Digby, somewhat unsettled by the exciting events that had occurred during the previous fortnight, had not slept as soundly as might have been expected after all his exertions. Now he dreamt of the shipwreck, then of his uncle's revolutionary movement. At times a woman's face appeared to him, a sad and melancholy face, with large and solemn eyes that looked reproachfully at the dreamer. Sir Richard Digby started several times, and would have addressed the apparition, holding out his hand as if to welcome it; but the phantom disappeared, and was immediately followed by visions of the jungle and by incidents of the wars in Africa. Now he was risking his life to save a hard-pressed comrade; and it seemed to him that what he had done had been performed less from a motive of gallantry than from a recklessness of his life, which had ceased to have any particular attraction for him.

Sir Richard moved uneasily on his couch, and presently awoke with racking pains in his head.

Going to the window, he threw open the casement, and admitted the fresh morning air, which cooled his temples. As he did so, the old clock in the turret struck three.

There were still two hours before dawn,

and he, remembering that as a boy he had often enjoyed capital trout-fishing in a stream that ran through the park, determined to take a rod, if one was to be found in the old place, and try his hand with the fly.

Having dressed, he proceeded to the river, and attaching his fly, commenced to whip the waters. By the pale light of the moon and stars, he could see in the distance the long lines of white tents that formed the camp of the soldiers. The massive old Castle stood out in the background, its turrets and towers cut clear and cold against the cloudless sky. That venerable pile had seen some startling episodes in the history of his country. It had been a haven of refuge to Charles I., on the eve of one of his encounters with Cromwell; and the very stream which ran before him, so white and clear that it reflected the moon upon its surface, had run red in the days gone by with the blood of Royalist and Republican.

On the very bed on which his weary limbs had found a fitful repose had rested the kingly head which fell beneath the stroke of the bloody axe.

The fish did not rise well, and Sir Richard, after whipping the water for about half an hour, put his rod down upon the ground, and resting himself against a great oak-tree, lit a pipe of tobacco. As he leaned forward to shield himself from the wind, a medallion fell from his pocket on the grass. He picked it up with an almost reverential touch, and opening it, gazed upon the picture it contained. The miniature which he held in his hand was that of a lady attired in Andalusian costume, such as even now may be seen at the balls in the Casino de Seville, after the

Holy Week, and during the celebrated fair. The portrait was painted, and the beautiful face before him, with its large clear eyes and olive skin, betokened her Spanish blood. The fan in her hand was so exquisitely designed that it seemed to shake as Sir Richard remembered he had seen it, when its owner had beckoned him towards her. What happy months they had spent together in the fair city on the Guadalquivir! Oh, those happy days, the days of their secret betrothal!—the rage of Ursula's father, the old marquis, when he discovered that his only child had secretly married a heretic—the night attack upon him near the arches of the great cathedral—how he had been left for dead by his assailants, and his fruitless search for his wife—all these memories flashed through his mind as he reclined against the tree, whilst the smoke from his pipe slowly curled upwards, caressed by the wanton wind.

Whilst thus dreaming, his attention was suddenly aroused by the sound of wheels. A carriage was ascending the road slowly, on account of the ground being very steep. The occupants, ignorant that they were observed, were talking freely to each other.

'Some Volunteers going to the encampment from the Castle, no doubt,' thought the Baronet, as he glanced through the trees that stood between his position and theirs.

'How heavy the old fellow's body is!' said one of the Volunteers; 'it is almost impossible to keep him upright.'

This observation reached Sir Richard's ears, and it excited his curiosity.

Peering round a tree, he saw a gig approaching, and two men inside it dressed as Volunteers, supporting a third, attired as a General. In another moment they passed by a bend in the road, within a few feet of the Baronet, when to his astonishment he recognised in the apparently inanimate figure his uncle, Lord Cromer. He at once realized that some treachery was at work, and his first impulse was to rush to the horse's head and arrest the carriage; but on second thoughts he remembered that he was single-handed, and without any means of defence. Moreover, he knew a short cut across the trout stream by which he could gain more than half a mile on the gig, and have the men arrested by the first patrol of Volunteers he fell in with. Allowing the carriage to pursue its course uninterrupted, he hastened down the bank of the stream, and springing from rock to rock, gained the opposite bank. Then, tightening his belt, he ran down the slope, keeping his body as near to the ground as possible, to avoid detection. Now he found himself in a morass up to his knees, then he had to penetrate a thick gorse cover; but regardless of difficulties he hurried on, until, on emerging from a plantation, he found himself on the high-road.

'The Volunteers' picket should be here,' he said to himself, 'if the man in charge has any knowledge of the country; for from this place there are five cross-paths, and the hollow below the plantation affords an admirable place for concealment.'

Digby looked around for the picket, but in vain; that which was so apparent to his practised eye had escaped the notice of the officer in charge of the outpost.

'Damn the fellow!' muttered Sir Richard; 'a nice sort of watch he keeps. I shall have to face it out with the scoundrels, for I can hear their wheels now.'

The place was not at all favourable for a single man to stop an enemy in the way. The Baronet felt sure that if he were to place himself in the middle of the road the driver would gallop his horse at him, and thus get the better of him in a moment.

He had nothing in his hand save the fishing-rod, which he had carried in the hope of its becoming useful. An idea occurred to him, which he put instantly into practice. He had been an enthusiastic fisherman, and could throw a fly with the greatest accuracy. Arranging his line and rod, and concealing himself behind the trunk of an old oak, he waited till the carriage arrived.

The horse was tired, from the uphill work he had been doing a greater part of the way, and was trotting slowly up the incline. As it reached the spot where Sir Richard was concealed, the Baronet threw his fly, which struck deep into the face of the driver, who, terrified and in great pain, instantly dropped the reins. Without wasting the tenth part of a second, Sir Richard rushed forward, and clubbing his fishing-rod, broke it upon the head of the other occupant of the carriage, at the same time calling out, as if he had some men behind him, 'Shoot the scoundrels—take good aim!'

The driver, who was maddened with pain and fear, tried to run away, followed by his companion, who escaped; but Sir Richard refused to relax his hold upon the line, and resolving to make a prisoner of one, wound the silk round his wrists, and threw him upon the ground. Finding some cord in the gig, he bound his man to a tree, and then, taking the reins, he jumped into the carriage and drove back to the Castle with all speed, supporting the prostrate form of his uncle with one arm.

On the road he met the officer in charge of the picket, and briefly relating what had occurred, ordered him to take a surgeon and release the prisoner from the tree, but to keep him in custody. He further charged the officer to send mounted men in pursuit of the other fugitive.

It was six o'clock by the time Sir Richard Digby reached the Castle. On the steps stood Sir Edward Righton in full uniform, surrounded by his staff. They were expecting Lord Cromer, and were expressing their surprise that he had not appeared. In a few words Digby explained what had occurred, and on investigating the matter, the ladder was found by which the men had entered the room.

The ablest surgeon in the camp was summoned, and on examining Lord Cromer he at once understood what had occurred. Indeed, the odour of the anæsthetic was still strong in the room, and the wound on Lord Cromer's arm showed where the drug had been injected. The surgeon, who had had great experience in the use of narcotics, used every possible means to restore his lordship. So successful was the treatment that in a few hours Lord Cromer opened his eyes, and was soon able to converse with those around his bed.

While Sir Richard Digby was standing in the room, an orderly brought him a despatch to the effect that the runaway had been secured, and placed in custody with the man whom Sir Richard had fastened to the tree. 'The men are so furious at the attempt made to capture Lord Cromer that I had great difficulty in preventing them from shooting the prisoners.'

'And it would have been what they well deserved,' thought Sir Richard Digby as he looked down the long lines of tents, and wondered how the campaign would end which had opened so inauspiciously.

16—2

CHAPTER XIX.

A LARGE party had assembled at the house of Mr. Sandford, the energetic Chief of the London Fire Brigade. Mr. Sandford was one of the most popular men in town. Respected by the lower classes, who admired such manly qualities as pluck and total abnegation of self, he was equally admired by the members of every club in Pall Mall. The result was that Mr. and Mrs. Sandford's 'at homes' were invariably well-attended, and fashionable dowagers with marriageable daughters would flock to his doors.

On this occasion there was something

decidedly original in the appearance of Mr. Sandford's house. The ground-floor, instead of consisting of a dining-room, library and smoking-room, as one usually finds in such houses, was entirely given up to the accommodation of model fire-engines. The brass fittings were brilliantly polished, and beneath the boilers prepared fuel was so arranged that it could be lit at a moment's notice. Gas-jets were always burning under the boilers, so that should a fire occur, by the time the horses were put-to the firemen would have no delay in getting up steam.

On the occasion of Mr. Sandford's evening parties these fire-engines were prettily decorated, and the hospitable Chief of the Fire Brigade spent much time in explaining the mechanism of the various engines to those who were interested in them. These little reunions had a peculiar charm of their own. There was no stiffness, and no one seemed bored. Although there was no lack of titled personages, the guests were not invited merely for their social position, but because they were representative people in the various walks of science, literature, and art. No man in London had a larger circle of acquaintance than the Chief of the London Fire Brigade.

In one room a number of telephones were placed, which communicated with every quarter of the Metropolis. Should a fire break out in any part of London, a bell would ring in this apartment, and information at once be communicated as to the nature of the conflagration. Orders would be immediately issued to the various inspectors under Mr. Sandford's command; and if the case was of sufficient urgency to need his immediate presence, he would at once proceed to the scene of the disaster.

Amongst Mr. and Mrs. Sandford's visitors on this occasion were Lady Tryington and her nieces, accompanied by Arthur Belper, who, although still weak, was gaining strength rapidly.

Lady Tryington had been obliged to go to town for a few days, after the arrival of the yacht at Holyhead, and Belper had accompanied them, to make his report of the shipwreck to the authorities. Mr. Metrale was also present, with Monsieur le Capitaine Victor Delange, the French Military Attaché, and even Ricardius was among the number of guests. Belper used frequently to be a visitor at the Sandfords', and on many occasions he had enjoyed the excitement of accompanying his friend at full speed to the scenes of some famous conflagrations, and had frequently exposed his life to danger in carrying out the commands of his friend.

'How elegantly Mr. Sandford has arrayed them,' said Blanche, to whom, much to Laura's annoyance, Arthur was explaining the mechanism of the fire-engines. 'It is a noble but a dangerous profession,' she continued; 'only second to that of a soldier.'

'Well, perhaps it is; but the men have been mostly sailors at some time, and are used to the climbing. Sandford, who is always the first to risk his own life when necessary, expects the same courage from his men, and secures it.'

'What splendid fellows sailors can be!' she observed. 'How nobly they behaved at the shipwreck, when, with your soldiers, the poor fellows perished!' She shuddered as she remembered how nearly Arthur Belper had shared their fate.

In the meantime, the French Attaché was conducting Lady Tryington and Laura to the room where the telephones were placed.

'It is so different in France,' he was saying to his companions. 'There, when a fire breaks out, soldiers march from both ends of the street, and force the people they meet to work in putting out the conflagration; whilst in this country there is no need of such pressure, and everyone seems eager to volunteer assistance.'

'Yes,' said Sandford, who had overheard the Attaché's last remark, 'they are so eager that they are often in the way. But we cannot afford to despise volunteers. Look at those helmets on the wall—they all belong to volunteers. That one, by the way,' he continued, 'belongs to a friend of yours, Captain Belper. He is one of the best men I have, and more particularly if there is any danger, for then he sets a splendid example to the less energetic and courageous.'

Blanche, who had entered the room as the chief was speaking of Belper, blushed with conscious pride as she heard him praised. At the same time she realized with fear how often he placed his life in peril; and then she knew how precious that life was to her.

At that moment one of the electric bells rang out clear and incessant, and the Chief of the Fire Brigade applied his ear to the telephone. He then signalled to his men in the engine-room, and without any fuss or commotion the horses were put to the engines. In less than five minutes he was in uniform, and, springing on to the foremost engine, was immediately followed by Arthur Belper and Victor Delange. For an instant Ricardius had imagined that he would like to be of the party; but considering that his pumps might get very wet, he sat down behind Blanche, who, pale and trembling at what had occurred, was listening to Lady Tryington's remarks.

Lady Tryington, who was a little angry at the sudden departure of her nieces' cavaliers, was telling Mrs. Sandford of the shipwreck, and of the marvellous escape of her nephew and Captain Belper.

'I hoped to have seen Sir Richard Digby here this evening,' said Mrs. Sandford; 'but men have always so many engagements.'

'He is not in London,' said Lady Tryington. 'He started for Meltingborough a few days ago, to visit some property he has in the neighbourhood.'

'Meltingborough!' said Ricardius; 'that dreadful place from which reports come that Lord Cromer intends to march on London?'

'I should not be surprised if Sir Richard joins his uncle,' said Lady Tryington.

'Sir Richard is too wise in his generation to commit himself in that way,' said Mr. Metrale. 'The Government is too strong to be so overturned. I have 15,000 men at my command, and we shall make an effectual resistance.'

'And while you are thus engaged,' remarked Mrs. Sandford, smiling, 'we shall be at the mercy of thieves and burglars.'

The party soon broke up after the departure of Mr. Sandford.

As Ricardius was stepping into his brougham, it occurred to him that he would like to see a little of the fire from a distance.

'Where is the fire?' said Ricardius to his coachman.

'At the Foreign Office, sir, Downing Street.'

CHAPTER XX.

'HOLD tight,' said Mr. Sandford to his friend the moment they reached the street.

The advice was not out of place, for the moment that the horses felt the reins slackened, they started forward at a gallop. Two firemen were standing behind, and shouting at the top of their voices, to warn people that the fire-engine was approaching.

'C'est magnifique!' said Victor Delange, as they darted through the streets at racing speed. 'How well the fellow drives!'

'He would not be here if he didn't do so,' said Sandford.

'Look, look!' exclaimed Victor Delange; 'the sky seems to be on fire.'

As they approached the scene of the conflagration, the sparks were shooting up through the clouds of smoke from the roof of the Foreign Office and the adjoining public buildings. A crash was heard, and there rose a vast crimson lake of fire to the heavens above, lighting up the faces of the crowds in the streets with a lurid glare.

'Great God!' exclaimed Sandford. 'It is serious. The Indian Office has caught as well.'

'The Prime Minister's residence, too,' said the driver.

'Look to your business,' called out the chief.

The mounted police were drawn up across the street, and were endeavouring to keep the crowd in order, and preventing them from passing the cord. The black helmets of the mounted police glowed beneath the light from the reflected flames, and their horses, from the excitement of the scene, became restive and unmanageable.

A cheer arose from the assembled crowds as the fire-engines came tearing down the street, and the crowd gave way to admit them to the front of the burning buildings.

END. OF VOL. I.

BILLING AND SONS, PRINTERS, GUILDFORD.
G., C. & Co.